'One of the most disturbing novels I've read in a long time. It possesses an unnerving air of documentary reality.'
Michiko Kakutani, *New York Times*

'An extremely traditional and very serious American novelist. He is the model of literary filial piety, counting among his parents Ernest Hemingway, F. Scott Fitzgerald, Nathanael West, and Joan Didion.'
Washington Post

'Never has Hollywood's version of success looked so frightening in a piece of contemporary literature.'
Newsday

'Remarkable. A killer—sexy, sassy, and sad. . . . It's a teenage slice-of-death novel, no holds barred. The feel of it hits where it hurts.'
Village Voice

'An extraordinarily accomplished first novel.'
New Yorker

LESS THAN ZERO

Bret Easton Ellis is the author of six novels, *Less Than Zero, The Rules of Attraction, American Psycho, Glamorama, Lunar Park* and most recently *Imperial Bedrooms*, which was a *Sunday Times* Top Ten Bestseller, and a collection of stories, *The Informers*. His work has been translated into thirty-two languages. He lives in Los Angeles.

BRET EASTON ELLIS

LESS THAN ZERO

With an introduction by
Ottessa Moshfegh

PICADOR CLASSIC

First published as a Borzoi Book 2010 by Alfred A. Knopf,
a division of Random House, Inc., New York
and simultaneously in Canada by Random House of Canada Limited, Toronto

First published in Great Britain 2010 by Picador

This Picador Classic edition first published 2019 by Picador
an imprint of Pan Macmillan
The Smithson, 6 Briset Street, London EC1M 5NR
Associated companies throughout the world
www.panmacmillan.com

ISBN 978-1-5098-7015-8

9 8 7 6 5 4

A CIP catalogue record for this book is available from the British Library.

Printed and bound by CPI Group (UK) Ltd, Croydon, CR0 4YY

Visit **www.picador.com** to read more about all our books
and to buy them. You will also find features, author interviews and
news of any author events, and you can sign up for e-newsletters
so that you're always first to hear about our new releases.

INTRODUCTION

TaB was introduced in 1963 as Coca-Cola's first diet soda. It used zero-calorie saccharin instead of sugar, an innovation that was intended to inspire people to indulge in carbonated sweetness without worrying about packing on the pounds. Finally, pleasure could be consumed without guilt, risk, or penalty. Forget water—here was a soda to make life carefree. Drink TaB and you were relinquished from mortal concern and responsibility, the ads suggested. More facetiously, commercials with skinny babes sucking down TaB sold consumers the idea that drinking it would actually make you thin. TaB was less than zero, in this sense. I remember first seeing TaB in movies in the '80s, when the drink rose to popularity. And it appears in *Less Than Zero* by Bret Easton Ellis with some frequency. Appropriately, within the first several pages, we hear that Muriel, a minor character, has been hospitalized for anorexia. TaB's nothingness seems central to the meaningless luxuries and woes of the youth generation in the '80s: immunity and ineffectuality are the highest privileges of the young, beautiful, and rich. *Less Than Zero* harnesses that ineffectuality with minimalism, pressurizing ennui into dread, and then into horror. Thus, it makes something out of nothing.

The novel's premise is simple: Clay, an eighteen-year-old college freshman, returns home to Los Angeles for winter break. His ex-girlfriend, Blair, picks him up from the airport and drives him home, where he is greeted by no one but a new housekeeper and the ripped poster of Elvis Costello on his bedroom wall. This is not LA at large, but a very specific gated land of multimillion-dollar homes, pool boys, private chefs, Lamborghinis, flawless skin, smog and diamonds, designer clothes, and narcissism so rampant it is considered the status quo. During his few weeks at home, Clay reconnects with old friends, parties, drives around, fools around with a guy and a few girls, remembers things, gets manipulated into loaning money to a friend who has to turn tricks to pay off a debt, the usual rich kid hijinks. To say that the youths are badly behaved would be to insinuate that there are well-behaved adults chasing them around with rulers. But the parents are absent, if not physically then certainly psychically, and the attitudes of both Clay's mother and father, who have broken up, seem not too far from their children's—aloof, corrupted, and disconnected. Everybody gossips, fucks, drives drunk. These are not *Beverly Hills, 90210* kids trying to manage social lives and please their parents with good grades. This is a higher stratum, one of derangement brought on by wealth earned in a culture where nothing is sacred. Entertainment and its exploitative industry always push consciousness into a void of indifference. Only the alchemical measures of human experience seem to relate: sex and drugs. So it is in *Less Than Zero*, where everybody's mom or dad is a film executive or a movie star, and their children are left to fend for themselves, with expensive cars and credit cards at their disposal.

The emotional valence of Clay's delivery is stark, a voice floating along with the smog and cigarette smoke. As the reader, I align myself with Clay, but Ellis still gets me to wonder whether Clay is on the inside or the outside of the nothingness. Clay's is not a pragmatic soul, but rather one that has been silenced through the oppression of lovelessness in his upbringing and the culture in which his persona has developed. Teetering between two worlds—New Hampshire, where he is a student, and Los Angeles—Clay seems to have maybe seen some light. Judgment cannot exist in a vacuum, after all. For the majority of the novel, Clay seems to harness the pacific patience of someone with nowhere better to be, no future, and no hope. But the velocity of his story—a high-speed with silent anxiety, zooming down the freeway doing a hundred miles per hour on downers listening to KNAC-FM—gives the terse hollowness of the narration its driving force. How Ellis managed to give Clay's voice the tension and weirdness that make this book unstoppable is beyond me as a writer. It is the calm one feels in the seconds before a car crash, just as you see the truck approaching and it's too late to switch lanes. The impeccable timing, especially in scenes of dialogue, captures the banalities of Clay's life in a way that both disgusts me and breaks my heart.

It seems against the rules of the book, canned and sappy, to point out the utter lack of love in it, such is the cage around its heart. Italicized sections throughout the novel narrate more emotional times in Palm Springs before Clay's grandmother dies, and even then, the world is flat, is tender-nessless. The past is smoke in the desert. It might haunt you, but it has no bearing on the purposelessness of your current existence. Clay has two sisters, but they too seem to be part of the system of drudgery and vanity. His dad takes Clay to dinners and treats him more like an underling or a frivolous employee than a beloved son. His mother is almost invisible in her blondness. She and Clay seem to have an under-standing that superficial communication avoids the painful territories of alienation and misery. As it renders the progeny of cold Hollywood elites as hot-bodied consumers and posers in pantomime of their greedy, aloof parents—snorting coke, doing lunch, getting drinks at the Polo Lounge at the Beverly Hills Hotel—*Less Than Zero* satirizes a world that feels both emblematic of the ills of the world in 1985, but also intensely personal. The lens of the narrator feels close to the author's. Perhaps that is my projection as a reader, one I make to explain how a voice so unaffected in its delivery could make my heart crash: I so badly want this world to be tethered to something real, to be the scratches on the prison walls, and for those marks to be rich with meaning. Expert satire func-tions this way; despite the straight read, we still identify and comprehend. It is not just a criticism of the world, but a full experience of it. With a little digging, I learn that Ellis's parents split in 1982. One must wonder how autobiograph-ical the novel really is. Not that it would change the impact of a novel, but the intimate knowledge of such a niche world begs the question.

I can only imagine the alienation this literary prodigy felt in a world that commodified art into entertainment meant to turn us into slaves of fashion and attitudes, to follow the programming of our film icons, to work hard to buy the right cars, to date the right people, to drink non-nutritive soft drinks, to sit and zone out in front of the TV. Only a bright young person can look at the contemporary world and see where it's going, unhinged from the static of the past. One political reading is to say that *Less Than Zero* functions as a condemnation of the evils of media. Los Angeles is a factory of illusion. It manufactures illusions, and creates an illusion around that manufacturing. Hollywood, which looks like shimmering magic from afar, is a complex system of egomaniacal executives responsible for feeding the masses narrative media, those box office hits we celebrate as the spawn of our cultural identity. Having grown up in Sherman Oaks, a neighborhood in the San Fernando Valley in Los Angeles, I assume that Ellis experienced this culture firsthand.

Less Than Zero came out in 1985, the same year TWA Flight 847 was hijacked by Hezbollah, Nintendo came out, and the Unabomber killed his first victim. Life-insurance companies began screening for AIDS. Compact discs were introduced. Reagan, a former actor deeply entrenched and corrupt in Hollywood politics, was President of the United States. The economic collapse of the middle class was romanticized in Hollywood for great profit, selling the trappings of suffering back to the people living the real deal with no exit strategy but their own eyes and ears affixed to the screens and radios. And to think, these were more innocent times! Decades later, with Trump in office, it seems that at times when there is an entertainer in the

White House, our culture descends into a lower realm of indecency—we lose track of what we mean by "humanity." The concept seems to come up only in the context of pain and death. Meanwhile, the division between art and entertainment becomes wonderfully clear. Entertainment is fodder for the masses, something to keep them busy and shopping while the world dies. Hollywood capitalizes on misery by canning culture and feeding it to us spoon by spoon. Art, on the other hand, is critical of the system of brainwashing, dehumanizing, consumerism, and greed. The difference between sincerity and satire is in the eye of the beholder. Someone with critical thinking can detect satire. Someone who is used to swallowing blindly whatever is served will never understand subtlety. I think this is why *Less Than Zero* was so controversial. The end of the book is the product of so much indifference. There's a dead kid in an alley that Clay's friends make into a spectacle, a twelve-year-old sex slave drugged and tied to a bed. These horrors are simply the actualization of exploitation which we all feel in abstraction through media, its hooks in our eye sockets. Clay, first running on the fumes of his habituated high-school patterns, begins to see his way out of the fog by the end of the novel. It's the shock of the dead kid or the twelve-year-old, or it's his self-disgust as a participant in passivity. The ambiguity is precise.

Subtlety has never been highly valued in mainstream culture. It is a necessary component of any satire, but not a prized quality in the US. We value outgoingness, aplomb, direct attacks, and celebrations. We favor straight arrows over innuendo. I think this is a weakness: when we take something at face value, we dismiss the deeper meaning. Satire, in my opinion, is the most difficult mode in literature because it functions with a delicate and invisible layer of self-awareness—self-awareness which readers themselves often lack. An insensitive reader of *Less Than Zero* might come away with the thought, "Well, that was disturbing," and point to the moments of vivid exploitation as "inappropriate" and "wrong." Such a reading does not appreciate the incredible timing, restraint, and synchronicity in the writing, nor the fact that these "inappropriate" scenes are actually a direct reflection of the reality we all live in. We often refuse to acknowledge the ugliness in ourselves and our world, out of shame or vanity.

I think the generative experience of reading this book is that of staring at a portrait of the human world—Los Angeles is its costume—for long enough that you see through the façade. The underbelly is always dark, but that darkness isn't what's so interesting to me. It's what the darkness is obscuring—a blank place unmarred by romanticism and sentimentalism, the hard truth. It is invisible because it is true. One must detach from the mundane activities of life to see this blankness, and this freedom. This is the beauty of *Less Than Zero*. The quiet transparency of existential terror is precisely what blew my mind. I am not horrified by a twelve-year-old girl drugged and tied to a bed while getting gang-raped. I'm horrified by the silence around it. If this book is an existential satire, its actual premise is that the world is hell disguised as paradise.

Ottessa Moshfegh

For Joe McGinniss

'This is the game that moves as you play . . .'

– X

'There's a feeling I get when I look to the West . . .'

– Led Zeppelin

LESS THAN ZERO

People are afraid to merge on freeways in Los Angeles. This is the first thing I hear when I come back to the city. Blair picks me up from LAX and mutters this under her breath as her car drives up the onramp. She says, 'People are afraid to merge on freeways in Los Angeles.' Though that sentence shouldn't bother me, it stays in my mind for an uncomfortably long time. Nothing else seems to matter. Not the fact that I'm eighteen and it's December and the ride on the plane had been rough and the couple from Santa Barbara, who were sitting across from me in first class, had gotten pretty drunk. Not the mud that had splattered the legs of my jeans, which felt kind of cold and loose, earlier that day at an airport in New Hampshire. Not the stain on the arm of the wrinkled, damp shirt I wear, a shirt which had looked fresh and clean this morning. Not the tear on the neck of my gray argyle vest, which seems vaguely more eastern than before, especially next to Blair's clean tight jeans and her pale-blue T-shirt. All of this seems irrelevant next to that one sentence. It seems easier to hear that people are afraid to merge rather than 'I'm pretty sure Muriel is anorexic' or the singer on the radio crying out about magnetic waves. Nothing else seems to matter to me but those ten words. Not the warm winds, which seem to propel the car down the empty asphalt freeway, or the faded smell of marijuana which still faintly permeates Blair's car. All it comes down to is that I'm a boy coming home for a month and meeting someone whom I haven't seen for four months and people are afraid to merge.

Blair drives off the freeway and comes to a red light. A heavy gust of wind rocks the car for a moment and Blair smiles and says something about maybe putting the top up and turns to a different radio station. Coming to my house, Blair has to stop the car since there are these five workmen lifting the remains of palm trees that have fallen during the winds and placing the leaves and pieces of dead bark in a big red truck, and Blair smiles again. She stops at my house and the gate's open and I get out of the car, surprised to feel how dry and hot it is. I stand there for a pretty long time and Blair, after helping me lift the suitcases out of the trunk, grins at me and asks, 'What's wrong?' and I say, 'Nothing,' and Blair says, 'You look pale,' and I shrug and we say goodbye and she gets into her car and drives away.

Nobody's home. The air conditioner is on and the house smells like pine. There's a note on the kitchen table that tells me that my mother and sisters are out, Christmas shopping. From where I'm standing I can see the dog lying by the pool, breathing heavily, asleep, its fur ruffled by the wind. I walk upstairs, past the new maid, who smiles at me and seems to understand who I am, and past my sisters' rooms, which still both look the same, only with different GQ cutouts pasted on the wall, and enter my room and see that it hasn't changed. The walls are still white; the records are still in place; the television hasn't been moved; the venetian blinds are still open, just as I had left them. It looks like my mother and the new maid, or maybe the old maid, cleaned out my closet while I was gone. There's a pile of comic books on my desk with a note on top of them that reads, 'Do you still want these?'; also a message that Julian called and a card that says 'Fuck Christmas' on it. I open it and it says 'Let's Fuck Christmas Together' on the inside, an invitation to Blair's Christmas party. I put the card down and notice that it's beginning to get really cold in my room.

I take my shoes off and lie on the bed and feel my brow to see if I have a fever. I think I do. And with my hand on my forehead I look up with caution at the poster encased in glass that hangs on the wall above my bed, but it hasn't changed either. It's the promotional poster for an old Elvis Costello record. Elvis looks past me, with this wry, ironic smile on his lips, staring out the window. The word 'Trust' hovering over his head, and his sunglasses, one lens red, the other blue, pushed down past the ridge of his nose so that you can see his eyes, which are slightly off center. The eyes don't look at me, though. They only look at whoever's standing by the window, but I'm too tired to get up and stand by the window.

I pick up the phone and call Julian, amazed that I actually can remember his number, but there's no answer. I sit up, and through the venetian blinds I can see the palm trees shaking wildly, actually bending, in the hot winds, and then I stare back at the poster and then turn away and then look back again at the smile and the mocking eyes, the red and blue glasses, and I can still hear people are afraid to merge and I try to get over the sentence, blank it out. I turn on MTV and tell myself I could get over it and go to sleep if I had some Valium and then I think about Muriel and feel a little sick as the videos begin to flash by.

I bring Daniel to Blair's party that night and Daniel is wearing sunglasses and a black wool jacket and black jeans. He's also wearing black suede gloves because he cut himself badly on a piece of glass a week earlier in New Hampshire. I had gone with him to the emergency room at the hospital and had watched as they cleaned the wound and washed the blood off and started to sew in the wire until I started feeling sick and then I went and sat in the waiting room at five o'clock in the morning and heard The Eagles sing 'New Kid in Town' and I wanted to come back. We're standing at the door of Blair's house in Beverly Hills and Daniel complains that the gloves are sticking to the wires and are too tight, but he doesn't take them off because he doesn't want people to see the thin silver wires sticking out of the skin on his thumb and fingers. Blair answers the door.

'Hey, gorgeous,' Blair exclaims. She's wearing a black leather jacket and matching pants and no shoes and she hugs me and then looks at Daniel.

'Well, who's this?' she asks, grinning.

'This is Daniel. Daniel, this is Blair,' I say.

Blair offers her hand and Daniel smiles and shakes it softly.

'Well, come on in. Merry Christmas.'

There are two Christmas trees, one in the living room and one in the den and both have twinkling dark-red lights coloring them. There are people at the party from high school, most of whom I haven't seen since graduation and they all stand next to the two huge trees. Trent, a male model I know, is there.

'Hey, Clay,' Trent says, a red-and-green-plaid scarf wrapped around his neck.

'Trent,' I say.

'How are you, babes?'

'Great. Trent, this is Daniel. Daniel, this is Trent.'

Trent offers his hand and Daniel smiles and adjusts his sunglasses and lightly shakes it.

'Hey, Daniel,' Trent says. 'Where do you go to school?'

'With Clay,' Daniel says. 'Where do you go?'

'U.C.L.A. or as the Orientals like to call it, U.C.R.A.' Trent imitates an old Japanese man, eyes slit, head bowed, front teeth stuck out in parody, and then laughs drunkenly.

'I go to the University of Spoiled Children,' Blair says,

still grinning, running her fingers through her long blond hair.

'Where?' asks Daniel.

'U.S.C.,' she says.

'Oh, yeah,' he says. 'That's right.'

Blair and Trent laugh and she grabs his arm to balance herself for a moment. 'Or Jew.S.C.,' she says, almost gasping.

'Or Jew.C.L.A.,' Trent says, still laughing.

Finally Blair stops laughing and brushes past me to the door, telling me that I should try the punch.

'I'll get the punch,' Daniel says. 'You want some, Trent?'

'No thanks.' Trent looks at me and says, 'You look pale.'

I notice that I do, compared to Trent's deep, dark tan and most of the other people's complexions around the room. 'I've been in New Hampshire for four months.'

Trent reaches into his pocket. 'Here,' he says, handing me a card. 'This is the address of a tanning salon on Santa Monica. Now, it's not artificial lighting or anything like that, and you don't have to rub Vitamin E capsules all over your bod. This thing is called an Uva Bath and what they do is they dye your skin.'

I stop listening to Trent after a while and look over at three boys, friends of Blair's I don't know, who go to U.S.C., all tan and blond and one is singing along with the music coming out of the speakers.

'It works,' Trent says.

'What works?' I ask, distracted.

'An Uva Bath. Uva Bath. Look at the card, dude.'

'Oh yeah.' I look at the card. 'They dye your skin, right?'

'Right.'

'Okay.'

Pause.

'What have you been doing?' Trent asks.

'Unpacking,' I say. 'What about you?'

'Well,' he smiles proudly. 'I got accepted by this modeling agency, a really good one,' he assures me. 'And guess who's going to be not only on the cover of *International Male* in two months, but who is also the month of June in U.C.L.A.'s college man calendar?'

'Who?' I ask.

'Me, dude,' Trent says.

'*International Male*?'

'Yeah. I don't like the magazine. My agent told them no nude stuff, just like Speedos and stuff like that. I don't do any nude stuff.'

I believe him but don't know why and look around the room to see if Rip, my dealer, is at the party. But I don't see him and I turn back to Trent and ask, 'Yeah? What else have you been doing?'

'Oh, like the usual. Going to Nautilus, getting smashed, going to this Uva place . . . But, hey, don't tell anyone I've been there, okay?'

'What?'

'I said don't tell anyone about this Uva place, okay?' Trent looks worried, concerned almost, and I put my hand on his shoulder and give it a squeeze to reassure him. 'Oh, yeah, don't worry.'

'Hey,' he says, looking around the room. 'Gotta do a little business. Later. Lunch,' he jokes, leaving.

Daniel comes back with the punch and it's very red and very strong and I cough a little as I take a swallow. From where I'm standing, I can see Blair's father, who's this movie producer and he's sitting in a corner of the den talking with this young actor I think I went to school with. Blair's father's boyfriend is also at the party. His name's Jared and he's really young and blond and tan and has blue eyes and incredibly straight white teeth and he's talking to the three boys from U.S.C. I can also see Blair's mother, who is sitting by the bar, drinking a vodka gimlet, her hands shaking as she brings the drink to her mouth. Blair's friend Alana comes into the den and hugs me and I introduce her to Daniel.

'You look just like David Bowie,' Alana, who is obviously coked up out of her mind, tells Daniel. 'Are you left-handed?'

'No, I'm afraid not,' Daniel says.

'Alana likes guys who are left-handed,' I tell Daniel.

'And who look like David Bowie,' she reminds me.

'And who live in the Colony,' I finish.

'Oh, Clay, you're such a beasty,' she giggles. 'Clay is a total beasty,' she tells Daniel.

'Yes, I know,' Daniel says. 'A beasty. Totally.'

'Have you had any punch? You should have some,' I tell her.

'Darling,' she says, slowly, dramatically. 'I made the punch.' She laughs and then spots Jared and stops suddenly. 'Oh, God, I wish Blair's father wouldn't invite Jared to these things. It makes her mother so nervous. She gets totally bombed anyway, but having him around makes it worse.' She turns to Daniel and says, 'Blair's mother is an agoraphobic.' She looks back at Jared. 'I mean he's going to Death Valley next week on location, I don't see why he can't wait until then, can you?' Alana turns to Daniel, then me.

'No,' Daniel says solemnly.

'Me neither,' I say, shaking my head.

Alana looks down and then back at me and says, 'You look kind of pale, Clay. You should go to the beach or something.'

'Maybe I will.' I finger the card Trent gave me and then ask her if Julian is going to show up. 'He called me and left a message, but I can't get in touch with him,' I say.

'Oh God, no,' Alana says. 'I hear he is like completely fucked up.'

'What do you mean?' I ask.

Suddenly the three boys from U.S.C. and Jared laugh loudly, in unison.

Alana rolls her eyes up and looks pained. 'Jared heard this stupid joke from his boyfriend who works at Morton's. "What are the two biggest lies?" "I'll pay you back and I won't come in your mouth." I don't even get it. Oh God, I better go help Blair. Mummy's going behind the bar. Nice to meet you, Daniel.'

'Yeah, you too,' Daniel says.

Alana walks over to Blair and her mother by the bar.

'Maybe I should have hummed a few bars of "Let's Dance,"' Daniel says.

'Maybe you should have.'

Daniel smiles. 'Oh Clay, you're such a total beasty.'

We leave after Trent and one of the boys from U.S.C. fall into the Christmas tree in the living room. Later that night, when the two of us are sitting at the end of the darkened bar at the Polo Lounge, not a whole lot is said.

'I want to go back,' Daniel says, quietly, with effort.

'Where?' I ask, unsure.

There's a long pause that kind of freaks me out and Daniel finishes his drink and fingers the sunglasses he's still wearing and says, 'I don't know. Just back.'

My mother and I are sitting in a restaurant on Melrose, and she's drinking white wine and still has her sunglasses on and she keeps touching her hair and I keep looking at my hands, pretty sure that they're shaking. She tries to smile when she asks me what I want for Christmas. I'm surprised at how much effort it takes to raise my head up and look at her.

'Nothing,' I say.

There's a pause and then I ask her, 'What do you want?'

She says nothing for a long time and I look back at my hands and she sips her wine. 'I don't know. I just want to have a nice Christmas.'

I don't say anything.

'You look unhappy,' she says real suddenly.

'I'm not,' I tell her.

'You look unhappy,' she says, more quietly this time. She touches her hair, bleached, blondish, again.

'You do too,' I say, hoping that she won't say anything else.

She doesn't say anything else, until she's finished her third glass of wine and poured her fourth.

'How was the party?'

'Okay.'

'How many people were there?'

'Forty. Fifty.' I shrug.

She takes a swallow of wine. 'What time did you leave it?'

'I don't remember.'

'One? Two?'

'Must've been one.'

'Oh.' She pauses again and takes another swallow.

'It wasn't very good,' I say, looking at her.

'Why?' she asks, curious.

'It just wasn't,' I say and look back at my hands.

I'm with Trent in a yellow train that sits on Sunset. Trent's smoking and drinking a Pepsi and I stare out the window and into the headlights of passing cars. We're waiting for Julian, who's supposed to be bringing Trent a gram. Julian is fifteen minutes late and Trent is nervous and impatient and when I tell him that he should deal with Rip, like I do, instead of Julian, he just shrugs. We finally leave and he says that we might be able to find Julian in the arcade in Westwood. But we don't find Julian at the arcade in Westwood, so Trent suggests that we go to Fatburger and eat something. He says he's hungry, that he hasn't eaten anything in a long time, mentions something about fasting. We order and take the food to one of the booths. But I'm not too hungry and Trent notices that there's no chili on my Fatburger.

'What is this? You can't eat a Fatburger without chili.'

I roll my eyes up at him and light a cigarette.

'Jesus, you're weird. Been up in fucking New Hampshire too long,' he mutters. 'No fucking chili.'

I don't say anything and notice that the walls have been painted a very bright, almost painful yellow and under the glare of the fluorescent lights, they seem to glow. Joan Jett and the Blackhearts are on the jukebox singing 'Crimson and Clover.' I stare at the walls and listen to the words. *'Crimson and clover, over and over and over and over . . .'* I suddenly get thirsty, but I don't want to go up to the counter and order anything because there's this fat, sad-faced Japanese girl taking orders and this security guard leaning against another yellow wall in back, eyeing everyone suspiciously, and Trent is still staring at my Fatburger with this amazed look on his face and there's this guy in a red shirt with long stringy hair, pretending to be playing the guitar and mouthing the words to the song in the booth next to ours and he starts to shake his head and his mouth opens. *'Crimson and clover, over and over and over . . . Crimson and clo-oh-ver . . .'*

It's two in the morning and hot and we're at the Edge in the back room and Trent is trying on my sunglasses and I tell him that I want to leave. Trent tells me that we'll leave soon, a couple of minutes maybe. The music from the dance floor seems too loud and I tense up every time the music stops and another song comes on. I lean back against the brick wall and notice that there are two boys embracing in a darkened corner. Trent senses I'm tense and says, 'What do you want me to do? You wanna lude, is that it?' He pulls out a Pez dispenser and pulls Daffy Duck's head back. I don't say anything, just keep staring at the Pez dispenser and then he puts it away and cranes his neck. 'Is that Muriel?'

'No, that girl's black.'

'Oh . . . you're right.'

Pause.

'It's not a girl.'

I wonder how Trent can mistake a black teenage boy, not anorexic, for Muriel, but then I see that the black boy is wearing a dress. I look at Trent and tell him again that I have to leave.

'Yeah, we all have to leave,' he says. 'You said that already.'

And so I stare at my shoes and Trent finds something to say. 'You're too much.' I keep staring at my shoes, tempted to ask him to let me see the Pez dispenser.

Trent says, 'Oh shit, find Blair, let's go, let's leave.'

I don't want to go back into the main room, but I realize you have to go through the main room to get back to the outside. I spot Daniel, who's talking to this really pretty tan girl who's wearing a Heaven cut-off T-shirt and a black-and-white miniskirt and I whisper to him that we're leaving and he gives me this look and says, 'Don't give me any shit.' I finally yank his arm and tell him he's really drunk and he says no kidding. He kisses the girl on the cheek and follows us toward the door, where Blair's standing, talking to some guy from U.S.C.

'Are we leaving?' she asks.

'Yeah,' I say, wondering where she's been.

We walk out into the hot night and Blair asks, 'Well, did we have a good time?' and nobody answers and she looks down.

Trent and Daniel are standing by Trent's BMW and Trent's pulling the Cliff Notes to *As I Lay Dying* out of his glove compartment and hands them to Blair. We say goodbye and make sure Daniel can get into his car. Trent says that maybe one of us should drive Daniel home but then agrees that it would be too much of a hassle to drive him home and then drive him back tomorrow. And I drive Blair back to her house in Beverly Hills and she fingers the Cliff Notes but doesn't say anything except when she tries to rub the stamp off her hand and she says, 'Fuck it. I wish they didn't have to stamp my hand in black. It never comes off.' And then she mentions that even though

I was gone for four months, I never called her. I tell her I'm sorry and turn off Hollywood Boulevard because it's too brightly lit and take Sunset and then drive onto her street and then to her driveway. We kiss and she notices that I've been gripping the steering wheel too hard and she looks at my fists and says, 'Your hands are red,' then gets out of the car.

We have been in Beverly Hills shopping most of the late morning and early afternoon. My mother and my two sisters and me. My mother has spent most of this time probably at Neiman-Marcus, and my sisters have gone to Jerry Magnin and have used our father's charge account to buy him and me something and then to MGA and Camp Beverly Hills and Privilege to buy themselves something. I sit at the bar at La Scala Boutique for most of this time, bored out of my mind, smoking, drinking red wine. Finally, my mother drives up in her Mercedes and parks the car in front of La Scala and waits for me. I get up and leave some money on the counter and get in the car and lean my head up against the headrest.

'She's going out with the biggest babe,' one of my sisters is saying.

'Where does he go to school?' the other one asks, interested.

'Harvard.'

'What grade is he in?'

'Ninth. One year above her.'

'I heard their house is for sale,' my mother says.

'I wonder if he's for sale,' the older of my two sisters, who I think is fifteen, mumbles, and both of them giggle from the backseat.

A truck with video games strapped in the back passes by and my sisters are driven into some sort of frenzy.

'Follow that video game!' one of them commands.

'Mom, do you think if I asked Dad he'd get me Galaga for Christmas?' the other one asks, brushing her short blond hair. I think she's thirteen, maybe.

'What is a Galaga?' my mother asks.

'A video game,' one of them says.

'You have Atari though,' my mother says.

'Atari's cheap,' she says, handing the brush to my other sister, who also has blond hair.

'I don't know,' my mother says, adjusting her sunglasses, opening the sunroof. 'I'm having dinner with him tonight.'

'That's encouraging,' the older sister says sarcastically.

'Where would we put it though?' one of them asks.

'Put what?' my mother asks back.

'Galaga! Galaga!' my sisters scream.

'In Clay's room, I suppose,' my mother says.

I shake my head.

'Bullshit! No way,' one of them yells. 'Clay can't have Galaga in his room. He always locks his door.'

'Yeah, Clay, that really pisses me off,' one of them says, a real edge in her voice.

'Why do you lock your door anyway, Clay?'

I don't say anything.

'Why do you lock your door, Clay?' one of them, I don't know which one, asks again.

I still don't say anything. I consider grabbing one of the bags from MGA or Camp Beverly Hills or a box of shoes from Privilege and flinging them out the window.

'Mom, tell him to answer me. Why do you lock your door, Clay?'

I turn around. 'Because you both stole a quarter gram of cocaine from me the last time I left my door open. That's why.'

My sisters don't say anything. 'Teenage Enema Nurses in Bondage' by a group called Killer Pussy comes on the radio, and my mother asks if we have to listen to this and my sisters tell her to turn it up, and no one says anything else until the song's over. When we get home, my younger sister finally tells me, out by the pool, 'That's bullshit. I can get my own cocaine.'

The psychiatrist I see during the four weeks I'm back is young and has a beard and drives a 450 SL and has a house in Malibu. I'll sit in his office in Westwood with the shades drawn and my sunglasses on, smoking a cigarette, some-times cloves, just to irritate him, sometimes crying. Sometimes I'll yell at him and he'll yell back. I tell him that I have these bizarre sexual fantasies and his interest will increase noticeably. I'll start to laugh for no reason and then feel sick. I lie to him sometimes. He'll tell me about his mistress and the repairs being done on the house in Tahoe and I'll shut my eyes and light another cigarette, gritting my teeth. Sometimes I just get up and leave.

I'm sitting in Du-par's in Studio City, waiting for Blair and Alana and Kim. They had called me and asked me to go to a movie with them, but I'd taken some Valium and had fallen asleep earlier that afternoon, and I couldn't get ready in time to meet them at the movie. So I told them I'd meet them at Du-par's. I'm sitting at a booth near a large window, and I ask the waitress for a cup of coffee, but she doesn't bring me anything, and she's already started to wipe the table next to mine and taken another table's order. But it's just as well that she doesn't bring me anything since my hands are shaking pretty badly. I light a cigarette and notice the big Christmas display above the main counter. A plastic, neon-lit Santa Claus is holding a three-foot-long Styrofoam candy cane and there are all these large green and red boxes leaning against it and I wonder if there's anything in the boxes. Eyes suddenly focus in on the eyes of a small, dark, intense-looking guy wearing a Universal Studios T-shirt sitting two booths across from me. He's staring at me and I look down and take a drag, a deep one, off the cigarette. The man keeps staring at me and all I can think is either he doesn't see me or I'm not here. I don't know why I think that. People are afraid to merge. *Wonder if he's for sale.*

Blair suddenly kisses me on the cheek and sits down along with Alana and Kim. Blair tells me that Muriel was hospitalized for anorexia today. 'She passed out in film class. So they took her to Cedars-Sinai which is not exactly the closest hospital to U.S.C.,' Blair says in a rush, lighting a cigarette. Kim is wearing pink sunglasses and she also lights one and then Alana asks for one.

'You are coming to Kim's party, Clay? Aren't you?' Alana asks.

'Oh yes, Clay. You've totally got to,' Kim says.

'When is it?' I ask, knowing that Kim always throws these parties, once a week or something like that.

'Sometime near the end of next week,' she tells me, though I realize that probably means tomorrow.

'I don't know who to go with,' Alana says suddenly. 'Oh, God, I don't know who the fuck to go with.' She pauses. 'I just realized that.'

'What about Cliff? Weren't you going with Cliff?' asks Blair.

'I'm going with Cliff,' Kim says, looking at Blair.

'Oh, that's right,' Blair says.

'Well, if you're going with Cliff, I'll go with Warren,' Alana says.

'But I thought you were going out with Warren,' Kim says to Blair.

I glance over at Blair.

'I was, but I'm not "going-out" with Warren,' Blair says, missing a beat.

'You were not. You fucked. You didn't "go-out,"' Alana says.

'Whatever, whatever,' Blair says, flipping through her menu, glancing over at me, then away.

'Did you sleep with Warren?' Kim asks Alana.

Alana looks at Blair and then at Kim and then at me and says, 'No. I didn't.' She looks back at Blair and then at Kim again. 'Did you?'

'No, but I thought Cliff was sleeping with Warren,' Kim says, confused for a moment.

'That might be true, but I thought Cliff was sleeping with that creepy Valley-turned-Punk, Didi Hellman,' says Blair.

'Oh, that is not true. Who told you that?' Alana wants to know.

I realize for an instant that I might have slept with Didi Hellman. I also realize that I might have slept with Warren also. I don't say anything. They probably already know.

'Didi did,' says Blair. 'Didn't she tell you that?'

'No,' Kim says. 'She didn't.'

'Me either,' Alana says.

'Well, she told me,' Blair says.

'Oh, what does she know? She lives in Calabasas for God's sakes,' Alana moans.

Blair thinks about it for a moment and then says slowly, evenly, 'If Cliff slept with Didi, then he must have slept with . . . Raoul.'

'Who's Raoul?' Alana and Kim ask at the same time.

I open my menu and pretend to read it, wondering if I slept with Raoul. Name seems familiar.

'Didi's other boyfriend. She was always getting into these disgusting threesomes. They were ridiculous,' Blair says, closing her menu.

'Didi is ridiculous,' says Alana.

'Raoul is black, isn't he?' Kim asks after a while.

I haven't slept with Raoul.

'Yeah. Why?'

'Because I think I met him at a backstage party at The Roxy once.'

'I thought he O.D.'d.'

'No, no. He's really cute. He's like the best-looking black guy I think I've ever seen,' Blair says.

Alana and Kim nod in agreement. I close my menu.

'But isn't he gay though?' Kim asks, looking concerned.

'Who? Cliff?' Blair asks.

'No. Raoul.'

'He's bi. Bi,' Blair says, and then, not too sure, 'I think.'

'I don't think he ever slept with Didi,' says Alana.

'Well, I really don't either,' Blair says.

'Then why did she go out with him?'

'She thought it was chic to have a black boyfriend,' Blair says, by now bored with the subject.

'What a sleaze,' Alana says, shivering in mock disgust.

The three of them stop talking and then Kim says, 'I had no idea Cliff slept with Raoul.'

'Cliff has slept with everyone,' Alana says, and rolls her eyes up, and Kim and Blair laugh. Blair looks at me and I try to smile and then the waitress comes and takes our order.

As I predicted, Kim's party is tonight. I follow Trent to the party. Trent's wearing a tie when he comes to my house and he tells me to wear one and so I put a red one on. When we stop at Santo Pietro's to get something to eat before the party, Trent catches his reflection in one of the windows and grimaces and takes his tie off and tells me to take mine off, which is just as well since no one at the party is wearing one.

At the house in Holmby Hills I talk to a lot of people who tell me about shopping for suits at Fred Segal and buying tickets for concerts and I hear Trent telling everyone about how much fun he's having at the fraternity he joined at U.C.L.A. I also talk to Pierce, some friend from high school, and apologize for not calling him when I got in and he tells me that it doesn't matter and that I look pale and that someone stole the new BMW his father bought him as a graduation present. Julian is at the party and he doesn't look as fucked up as Alana said: still tan, hair still blond and short, maybe a little too thin, but otherwise looks good. Julian tells Trent that he's sorry he missed him at Carney's the other night and that he's been really busy and I'm standing next to Trent, who has just finished his third gin and tonic, and hear him say, 'That's just really fucking irresponsible of you,' and I turn away, wondering if I should ask Julian what he wanted when he called and left the message, but when our eyes meet and we're about to say hello, he looks away and walks into the living room. Blair dances over to me, singing the words to 'Do You Really Want to Hurt Me?' probably stoned out of her mind, and she says that I look happy and that I look good and she hands me a box from Jerry Magnin and whispers 'Merry Christmas, you fox,' in my ear, and kisses me.

I open the box. It's a scarf. I thank her and tell her that it's really nice. She tells me to put it on and see if it fits and I tell her that scarves usually fit all people. But she insists and I put the scarf on and she smiles and murmurs 'Perfect' and goes back to the bar to get a drink. I stand alone with the scarf wrapped around my neck in the corner of the living room and then spot Rip, my dealer, and am totally relieved.

Rip's wearing this thick, bulky white outfit he probably bought at Parachute, and an expensive black fedora, and Trent asks Rip, as he makes his way toward me, if he's been going parachuting. 'Going Parachuting? Get it?' Trent says, giggling. Rip just stares at Trent until Trent stops giggling. Julian comes back into the room and I'm about to go over and say hello, but Rip grabs the scarf around my neck and pulls me into an empty room. I notice that there's no furniture in the room and begin to wonder why; then Rip hits me lightly on the shoulder and laughs.

'How the fuck have you been?'

'Great,' I say. 'Why is there no furniture in here?'

'Kim's moving,' he says. 'Thanks for returning my phone call, you dick.'

I know that Rip hasn't tried to call me, but I say, 'Sorry, I've only been back like four days and . . . I don't know . . . But I've been looking for you.'

'Well, here I am. What can I do for you, dude?'

'What have you got?'

'What did you take up there?' Rip asks, not really interested in answering me. He takes two small folded envelopes out of his pocket.

'Well, an art course and a writing course and this music course —'

'Music course?' Rip interrupts, pretending to get excited. 'Did you write any music?'

'Well, yeah, a little.' I reach into my back pocket for my wallet.

'Hey, I got some lyrics. Write some music. We'll make millions.'

'Millions of what?'

'Are you going back?' Rip asks, not missing a beat.

I don't say anything, just stare at the half gram he's poured onto a small hand mirror.

'Or are you gonna stay . . . and play . . . in L.A.' Rip laughs and lights a cigarette. With a razor he cuts the pile into four big lines and then he hands me a rolled up twenty and I lean down and do a line.

'Where?' I ask, lifting my head up, sniffing loudly.

'Jesus,' Rip says, leaning down. 'To school, you jerk.'

'I don't know. I suppose so.'

'You suppose so.' He does both his lines, huge, long lines, and then hands me the twenty.

'Yeah,' I shrug, leaning back down.

'Cute scarf. Real cute. Guess Blair still likes you,' Rip smiles.

'I guess,' I say, doing the other long line.

'You guess, you guess,' Rip laughs.

I smile and shrug again. 'It's good. How about a gram?'

'Here you go, dude.' He hands me one of the small envelopes.

I give him two fifties and a twenty and he hands me the twenty back and says, 'Christmas present, okay?'

'Thanks a lot, Rip.'

'Well, I think you should go back,' he says, pocketing the money. 'Don't fuck off. Don't be a bum.'

'Like you?' I regret saying this. It comes out wrong.

'Like me, dude,' Rip says, missing a beat.

'I don't know if I want to,' I begin.

'What do you mean, you don't know if you want to?'

'I don't know. Things aren't that different there.'

Rip is getting restless and I get the feeling that it doesn't matter a whole lot to Rip whether I stay or go.

'Listen, you've got a long vacation, don't you? A month, right?'

'Yeah. Four weeks.'

'A month, right. Think about it.'

'I'll do that.'

Rip walks over to the window.

'Are you deejaying anymore?' I ask, lighting a cigarette.

'No way, man.' He runs his finger over the mirror and rubs it over his teeth and gums, then slips the mirror back into his pocket. 'The trust is keeping things steady for now. I might go back when I run out. Only problem is, I don't think it's ever gonna run out,' he laughs. 'I got this totally cool penthouse on Wilshire. It's fantastic.'

'Really?'

'Yeah. You gotta stop by.'

'I will.'

Rip sits on the windowsill and says, 'I think Alana wants to fuck me. What do you think?'

I don't say anything. I can't understand why since Rip doesn't look anything like David Bowie, he's not left-handed and doesn't live in the Colony.

'Well, should I fuck her or what?'

'I don't know,' I say. 'Sure, why not?'

Rip gets off the windowsill and says, 'Listen, you've got to come over to the apartment. I got *Temple of Doom* bootleg. Cost me four hundred dollars. You should come over, dude.'

'Yeah, sure, Rip.' We walk to the door.

'You will?'

'Why not.'

When the two of us enter the living room these two girls who I don't remember come up to me and tell me I should give them a call and one of them reminds me about the night at The Roxy and I tell her that there have been a lot of nights at The Roxy and she smiles and tells me to call her anyway. I'm not sure if I have this girl's number and just as I'm about to ask her for it, Alana walks up to me and tells me that Rip has been bothering her and is there anything I can do about it? I tell her I don't think so. And as Alana starts to talk about Rip, I watch Rip's roommate dance with Blair next to the Christmas tree. He whispers something into her ear and they both laugh and nod their heads.

There's also this old guy with longish gray hair and a Giorgio Armani sweater and moccasins on who wanders past Alana and me and he begins to talk to Rip. One of the boys from U.S.C. who was at Blair's party is also here and he looks at the old man, guy maybe forty, forty-five, and then turns to one of the girls who met me at The Roxy and makes a face. He notices me looking at him when he does this and he smiles and I smile back and Alana keeps going on and on and luckily someone turns the volume up and Prince starts to scream. Alana leaves once a song she wants to dance to comes on, and this guy from U.S.C., Griffin, comes up to me and asks if I want some champagne. I tell him sure and he goes to the bar and I look for a bathroom to do another line.

I have to go through Kim's room to get to it, since the lock on the one downstairs is broken, and as I get to her door, Trent comes out and closes it.

'Use the one downstairs,' he says.

'Why?'

'Because Julian and Kim and Derf are fucking in there.'

I just stand there. 'Derf's here?' I ask.

'Come with me,' Trent says.

I follow Trent downstairs and out of the house and over to his car.

'Get in,' he says.

I open the door and get into the BMW.

'What do you want?' I ask him as he gets in on the driver's side.

He reaches into his pocket and pulls out a small vial.

'A little co-kaine,' he says in a fake southern drawl.

I don't tell him I already have some and he takes out a gold spoon and presses the spoon into the powder and then holds it up to his nose and does this four times. He then pushes the same tape that is on at the party into the car's stereo and hands me the vial and the spoon. I do four hits also and my eyes water and I swallow. It's different coke than Rip's and I wonder if he got it from Julian. It's not as good.

'Why don't we go to Palm Springs for a week while you're back,' he suggests.

'Yeah. Palm Springs. Sure,' I tell him. 'Listen, I'm going back in.'

I leave Trent alone in the car and walk back to the party and over toward the bar, where Griffin is standing, holding two glasses of champagne. 'I think it's a little flat,' he says.

'What?'

'I said your champagne's flat.'

'Oh.' I pause, confused for a minute. 'That's all right.'

I drink it anyway and he pours me another glass.

'It's still pretty good,' he says after finishing his glass and pouring himself another. 'Want some more?'

'Sure.' I finish my second glass and he pours me a third. 'Thanks.'

'The girl I came with just left with that Japanese guy in the English Beat T-shirt and tight white pants. You know who he is?'

'No.'

'Kim's hairdresser.'

'Wild,' I say, finishing the glass of champagne and looking at Blair from across the room. Our eyes meet and she smiles and makes a face. I smile back, don't make a face. Griffin notices this and says loudly, over the din of the music, 'You're the guy who's going out with Blair, right?'

'Well, used to go out with her.'

'I thought you still were.'

'Maybe we are,' I say, pouring another glass of champagne. 'I don't know.'

'She talks about you a lot.'

'Really? Well . . .' My voice trails off.

We don't say anything for a long time.

'Like your scarf,' Griffin says.

'Thanks.' I drain the glass and pour myself another, and wonder what time it is and how long I've been here. The coke is wearing off and I'm starting to get a little drunk.

Griffin takes a deep breath and says, 'Hey, you wanna go to my house? Parents are in Rome for Christmas.' Someone changes a tape and I sigh and look at the glass of champagne he's holding, then finish my glass fast and say sure, why not.

Griffin stands by his bedroom window, looking out into the backyard, at the pool, only wearing a pair of jockey shorts and I'm sitting on the floor, my back leaning against his bed, bored, sober, smoking a cigarette. Griffin looks at me and slowly, clumsily, pulls off his underwear and I notice that he doesn't have a tan line and I begin to wonder why and almost laugh.

I wake up sometime before dawn. My mouth is really dry and it hurts to unstick my tongue from the roof of my mouth. I close my eyes tightly and try to go back to sleep, but the digital clock on the nightstand says that it's four-thirty and I only now fully realize where I am. I look over at Griffin, lying on the other side of the big double bed. I don't want to wake Griffin up, so I get out of the bed as carefully as possible and walk into the bathroom and close the door. I take a piss and then stare at myself, nude, in the mirror for a moment, and then lean against the sink and turn on the faucet and splash cold water on my face. Then I look at myself in the mirror again, this time longer. I go back into the bedroom and put my underwear on, making sure they're not Griffin's, then I look around the room and panic, because I can't find my clothes. Then I remember that it started in the living room last night, and I quietly walk down the stairs of the huge, empty mansion and into the living room. I find my clothes and dress quickly. As I'm pulling my pants up, this black maid, wearing a blue robe, hair in curlers, passes by the door and glances at me for a moment, casually, as if finding some young guy, eighteen or whatever, pulling up his pants in the middle of the living room at five in the morning was not weird. She leaves and I have trouble finding the front door. After I do find it and leave the house, I tell myself that it really wasn't that bad last night. And I get into the car and open the glove compartment and cut a line, just to make it home. Then I drive past the gates of the house and onto Sunset.

I turn the radio up, loud. The streets are totally empty and I drive fast. I come to a red light, tempted to go through it, then stop once I see a billboard that I don't remember seeing and I look up at it. All it says is 'Disappear Here' and even though it's probably an ad for some resort, it still freaks me out a little and I step on the gas really hard and the car screeches as I leave the light. I put my sunglasses on even though it's still pretty dark outside and I keep looking into the rearview mirror, getting this strange feeling that someone's following me. I come to another red light and that's when I realize that I forgot the scarf Blair gave me; left it at Griffin's.

My house lies on Mulholland and as I press the gate opener, I look out over the Valley and watch the beginning of another day, my fifth day back, and then I pull into the circular driveway and park my car next to my mother's, which is parked next to a Ferrari that I don't recognize. I sit there and listen to the last lines of some song and then get out of the car and walk to the front door and find my key and open it. I walk upstairs to my bedroom and lock the door and light a cigarette and turn the television on and turn the sound off and then I walk into the closet and find the bottle of Valium that I hid beneath some cashmere sweaters. After looking at the small yellow pill with the hole in the middle of it, I decide that I really don't need it and I put it away. I take off my clothes and look at the digital clock, the same kind of digital clock that Griffin has, and notice that I only have a few hours to sleep before I have to meet my father for lunch, so I make sure the alarm is set and I lay back, staring at the television hard, because I once heard that if you stare at the television screen for a long enough time, you can fall asleep.

The alarm goes off at eleven. A song called 'Artificial Insemination' is playing on the radio and I wait until it's over to open my eyes and get up. Sun is flooding the room through the venetian blinds and when I look in the mirror it gives the impression that I have this wild, cracked grin. I walk into the closet and look at my face and body in the mirror; flex my muscles a couple of times, wonder if I should get a haircut, decide I do need a tan. Turn away and open the envelope, also hid beneath the sweaters. I cut myself two lines of the coke I bought from Rip last night and do them and feel better. I'm still wearing my jockey shorts as I walk downstairs. Even though it's eleven, I don't think anyone is up yet and I notice that my mother's door is closed, probably locked. I walk outside and dive into the pool and do twenty quick laps and then get out, towel myself dry as I walk into the kitchen. Take an orange from the refrigerator and peel it as I walk upstairs. I eat the orange before I get into the shower and realize that I don't have time for the weights. Then I go into my room and turn on MTV really loud and cut myself another line and then drive to meet my father for lunch.

I don't like driving down Wilshire during lunch hour. There always seem to be too many cars and old people and maids waiting for buses and I end up looking away and smoking too much and turning the radio up to full volume. Right now, nothing is moving even though the lights are green. As I wait in the car, I look at the people in the cars next to mine. Whenever I'm on Wilshire or Sunset during lunch hour I try to make eye contact with the driver of the car next to mine, stuck in traffic. When this doesn't happen, and it usually doesn't, I put my sunglasses back on and slowly move the car forward. As I pull onto Sunset I pass the billboard I saw this morning that read 'Disappear Here' and I look away and kind of try to get it out of my mind.

My father's offices are in Century City. I wait around for him in the large, expensively furnished reception room and hang out with the secretaries, flirting with this really pretty blond one. It doesn't bother me that my father leaves me waiting there for thirty minutes while he's in some meeting and then asks me why I'm late. I don't really want to go out to lunch today, would rather be at the beach or sleeping or out by the pool, but I'm pretty nice and I smile and nod a lot and pretend to listen to all his questions about college and I answer them pretty sincerely. And it doesn't embarrass me a whole lot that while on the way to Ma Maison he puts the top of the 450 down and plays a Bob Seger tape, as if this was some sort of weird gesture of communication. It also doesn't really make me angry that at lunch my father talks to a lot of businessmen, people he deals with in the film industry, who stop by our table and that I'm introduced only as 'my son' and the businessmen all begin to look the same and I begin to wish that I had brought the rest of the coke.

My father looks pretty healthy if you don't look at him for too long. He's completely tan and has had a hair transplant in Palm Springs, two weeks ago, and he has pretty much a full head of blondish hair. He also has had his face lifted. I'd gone to see him at Cedars-Sinai when he had it done and I remember seeing his face covered with bandages and how he would keep touching them lightly.

'Why aren't you having the usual?' I ask, actually interested, after we order.

He smiles, showing off the caps. 'Nutritionist won't allow it.'

'Oh.'

'How is your mother?' he asks calmly.

'She's fine.'

'Is she really feeling fine?'

'Yes, she's really feeling fine.' I'm tempted, for a moment, to tell him about the Ferrari parked in the driveway.

'Are you sure?'

'There's nothing to worry about.'

'That's good.' He pauses. 'Is she still seeing that Dr. Crain?'

'Uh-huh.'

'That's good.'

There's a pause. Another businessman stops by, then leaves.

'Well, Clay, what do you want for Christmas?'

'Nothing,' I say after a while.

'Do you want your subscription to *Variety* renewed?'

'It already is.'

Another pause.

'Do you need money?'

'No,' I tell him, knowing that he'll slip me some later on, outside Ma Maison maybe, or on the way back to his office.

'You look thin,' he says.

'Hmmm.'

'And pale.'

'It's the drugs,' I mumble.

'I didn't quite hear that.'

I look at him and say, 'I've gained five pounds since I've been back home.'

'Oh,' he says, and pours himself a glass of white wine.

Some other business guy drops by. After he leaves, my father turns to me and asks, 'Do you want to go to Palm Springs for Christmas?'

During the end of my senior year one day, I didn't go to school. Instead I drove out to Palm Springs alone and listened to a lot of old tapes I used to like but didn't much anymore, and I stopped at a McDonald's in Sunland for a Coke and then drove out to the desert and parked in front of the old house. I didn't like the new one that the family had bought; well, it was okay, but it wasn't like the old house. The old house was empty and the outside looked really scummy and unkempt and there were weeds and a television aerial that had fallen off the roof and empty trash cans were lying on what used to be the front lawn. The pool was drained and all these memories rushed back to me and I had to sit down in my school uniform on the steps of the empty pool and cry. I remembered all the Friday nights driving in and the Sunday nights leaving and afternoons spent playing cards on the chaise longues out by the pool with my grandmother. But those memories seemed faded compared to empty beer cans that were scattered all over the dead lawn and the windows that were all smashed and broken. My aunt had tried to sell the house, but I guess she got sentimental and no longer wanted to. My father had wanted to sell it and was really bitter that no one had done so. But they stopped talking about it and the house lay between them and was never brought up anymore. I didn't go out to Palm Springs that day to look around or see the house and I didn't go because I wanted to miss school or anything. I guess I went out there because I wanted to remember the way things were. I don't know.

On the way home from lunch, I stop by Cedars-Sinai to visit Muriel, since Blair told me that she really wanted to see me. She's really pale and so totally thin that I can make out the veins in her neck too clearly. She also has dark circles under her eyes and the pink lipstick she's put on clashes badly with the pale white skin on her face. She's watching some exercise show on TV and all these issues of *Glamour* and *Vogue* and *Interview* lie by her bed. The curtains are closed and she asks me to open them. After I do, she puts her sunglasses on and tells me that she's having a nicotine fit and that she's 'absolutely dying' for a cigarette. I tell her I don't have any. She shrugs and turns the volume up on the television and laughs at the people doing the exercises. She doesn't say that much, which is just as well since I don't say much either.

I leave the parking lot of Cedars-Sinai and make a couple of wrong turns and end up on Santa Monica. I sigh, turn up the radio, some little girls are singing about an earthquake in L.A. *'My surfboard's ready for the tidal wave.'* A car pulls up next to mine at the next light and I turn my head to see who's in it. Two young guys in a Fiat and both have short hair and bushy mustaches and are wearing plaid short-sleeve shirts and ski vests and one looks at me, with this total look of surprise and disbelief and he tells his friend something and now both of them are looking at me. *'Smack, smack, I fell in a crack.'* The driver rolls down his window and I tense up and he asks me something, but my window's rolled up and the top isn't down and so I don't answer his question. But the driver asks me again, positive that I'm this certain actor. *'Now I'm part of the debris,'* the girls are squealing. The light turns green and I drive away, but I'm in the left-hand lane and it's a Friday afternoon nearing five and the traffic's bad, and when I come to another red light, the Fiat's next to me again, and these two insane fags are laughing and pointing and asking me the same fucking question over and over. I finally make an illegal left turn and come to a side street, where I park for a minute and turn the radio off, light a cigarette.

Rip's supposed to meet me at Cafe Casino in Westwood, and he hasn't shown up yet. There's nothing to do in Westwood. It's too hot to walk around and I've seen all the movies, some even twice, and so I sit under the umbrellas at Cafe Casino and drink Perrier and grapefruit juice and watch the cars roll by in the heat. Light a cigarette and stare at the Perrier bottle. Two girls, sixteen, seventeen, both with short hair, sit at the table next to mine and I keep looking over at both of them and they both flirt back; one's peeling an orange and the other's sipping an espresso. The one who's peeling an orange asks the other if she should put a maroon streak through her hair. The girl with the espresso takes a sip and tells her no. The other girl asks about other colors, about anthracite. The girl with the espresso takes another sip and thinks about this for a minute and then tells her no, that it should be red, and if not red, then violet, but definitely not maroon or anthracite. I look over at her and she looks at me and then I look at the Perrier bottle. The girl with the espresso pauses a couple of seconds and then asks, 'What's anthracite?'

A black Porsche with tinted windows pulls up in front of Cafe Casino and Julian gets out. He sees me and, though it looks like he doesn't want to, comes over. His hand falls on my shoulder and I shake his other hand.

'Julian,' I say. 'How've you been?'

'Hey, Clay,' he says. 'What's going on? How long have you been back?'

'Just like five days,' I say. Just five days.

'What are you doing?' he asks. 'What's going on?'

'I'm waiting for Rip.'

Julian looks really tired and kind of weak, but I tell him he looks great and he says that I do too, even though I need to get a tan.

'Hey, listen,' he starts. 'I'm sorry about not meeting you and Trent at Carney's that night and freaking out at the party. It's just like, I've been strung out for like the past four days, and I just, like, forgot . . . I haven't even been home . . .' He slaps his forehead. 'Oh man, my mother must be freaking out.' He pauses, doesn't smile. 'I'm just so sick of dealing with people.' He looks past me. 'Oh shit, I don't know.'

I look over at the black Porsche and try to see past the tinted windows and begin to wonder if there's anyone else in the car. Julian starts playing with his keys.

'Do you want something, man?' he asks. 'I mean, I like you and if you need anything, just come see me, okay?'

'Thanks. I don't need anything, not really.' I stop and feel kind of sad. 'Jesus, Julian, how have you been? We've got to get together or something. I haven't seen you in a long time.' I stop. 'I've missed you.'

Julian stops playing with his keys and looks away from me. 'I've been all right. How was . . . oh shit, where were you, Vermont?'

'No, New Hampshire.'

'Oh yeah. How was it?'

'Okay. Heard you dropped out of U.S.C.'

'Oh yeah. Couldn't deal with it. It's so totally bogus. Maybe next year, you know?'

'Yeah . . .' I say. 'Have you talked to Trent?'

'Oh man, if I want to see him, I'll see him.'

There's another pause, this time longer.

'What have you been doing?' I finally ask.

'What?'

'Where have you been? What've you been doing?'

'Oh, I don't know. I've been around. Went to that Tom Petty concert at the . . . Forum. He sang that song, oh, you know, that song we always used to listen to . . .' Julian closes his eyes and tries to remember the song. 'Oh, shit, you know . . .' He begins to hum and then sing the words. '*Straight into darkness, we went straight into darkness, out over that line, yeah straight into darkness, straight into night . . .*'

The two girls look over at us. I look at the Perrier bottle, a little embarrassed, and say, 'Yeah, I remember.'

'Love that song,' he says.

'Yeah, so did I,' I say. 'What else you been up to?'

'No good,' he laughs. 'Oh, I don't know. Just been hanging out.'

'You called me and left a message, didn't you?'

'Oh, yeah.'

'What did you want?'

'Oh forget it, nothing too important.'

'Come on, what is it?'

'I said forget it, Clay.'

He takes off his sunglasses and squints and his eyes

look blank, and the only thing I can think of to say is, 'How was the concert?'

'What?' He starts to bite his nails.

'The concert. How was it?'

He's staring off somewhere else. The two girls get up and leave.

'It was a bummer, man. A real fuckin' bummer,' he finally says, and then walks away. 'Later.'

'Yeah, later,' I say, and look back at the Porsche and get the feeling that there's someone else in it.

Rip never shows up at Cafe Casino and he calls me up, later, around three and tells me to come over to the apartment on Wilshire. Spin, his roommate, is sunbathing nude on the balcony and Devo's on the stereo. I walk into Rip's bedroom and he's still in bed, nude, and there's a mirror on the nightstand, next to the bed, and he's cutting a line of coke. And he tells me to come in, sit down, check the view out. I walk over to the window and he gestures at the mirror and asks if I want any coke and I tell him I don't think so, not now.

A very young guy, probably sixteen, maybe fifteen, really tan, comes out of the bathroom and he's zipping up his jeans and buckling his belt. He sits on the side of the bed and puts on his boots, which seem too big for him. This kid has really short, spiked blond hair and a Fear T-shirt on and a black leather bracelet strapped to one of his wrists. Rip doesn't say anything to him and I pretend that the kid isn't there. He stands up and stares at Rip and then leaves.

From where I'm sitting, I watch as Spin gets up and walks into the kitchen, still nude, and starts to squeeze grapefruits into a large glass container. He calls to Rip, from the kitchen, 'Did you make reservations wth Cliff at Morton's?'

'Yeah, babes,' Rip calls back, before doing the coke.

I'm beginning to wonder why Rip has called me over, why he couldn't meet me someplace else. There's an old, expensively framed poster of The Beach Boys hanging over Rip's bed and I stare at it trying to remember which one died, while Rip does three more lines. Rip throws his head back and shakes it and sniffs loudly. He then looks at me and wants to know what I was doing at the Cafe Casino in Westwood when he clearly remembers telling me to meet him at the Cafe Casino in Beverly Hills. I tell him that I'm pretty sure he said to meet at the Cafe Casino in Westwood.

Rip says, 'No, not quite,' and then, 'Anyway it doesn't matter.'

'Yeah, I guess.'

'What do you need?'

I pull my wallet out and get the feeling that Rip never showed up at the Cafe Casino in Beverly Hills either.

Trent's on the phone in his room, trying to score some coke from a dealer who lives in Malibu since he hasn't been able to get in touch with Julian. After talking to the guy for like twenty minutes he hangs the phone up and looks at me. I shrug and light a cigarette. The telephone keeps ringing and Trent keeps telling me that he'll go see a movie, any movie, with me in Westwood since something like nine new films opened Friday. Trent sighs and then answers the phone. It's the new dealer. The phone call is not good. Trent hangs up and I mention that maybe we should leave, see a four o'clock show. Trent tells me that maybe I should go with Daniel or Rip or one of my 'faggot friends.'

'Daniel's not a faggot,' I say, bored, turning the channel on the television.

'Everyone thinks he is.'

'Like who?'

'Like Blair.'

'Well, he isn't.'

'Try telling that to Blair.'

'I'm not going out with Blair anymore. That is over, Trent,' I tell him, trying to sound steady.

'I don't think she thinks so,' Trent says, lying back on the bed, staring at the ceiling.

Finally, I ask, 'Why do you even care?'

'Maybe I don't,' he sighs.

Trent changes the subject and tells me I should go with him to a party someone's having for some new group at The Roxy. I ask who's giving it and he tells me he's not too sure.

'What group is it for?' I ask.

'Some new group.'

'Which new group?'

'I don't know, Clay.'

The dog begins to bark loudly from downstairs.

'Maybe,' I tell him. 'Daniel's having a party tonight.'

'Oh great,' he says sarcastically. 'A fag party.'

The phone rings again. 'Screw you,' I say.

'Jesus!' Trent yells, sitting up, grabbing the telephone and screaming into it, 'I don't even want your lousy, fucking coke!' He pauses for a moment and then says, 'Yeah, I'll be right down.' He hangs the phone up and looks at me.

'Who was it?'

'My mother. She's calling from downstairs.'

We walk downstairs. The maid's sitting in the living room, with this dazed look on her face, watching MTV. Trent tells me that she doesn't like to clean the house when anybody's home. 'She's always stoned anyway. Mom feels guilty since her family was killed in El Salvador, but I think she'll fire her sooner or later.' Trent walks over to the maid and she looks up nervously and smiles. Trent tries some of his Spanish but can't communicate with her. She just looks at him blankly and tries to nod and smile. Trent turns around and says, 'Yep, stoned again.'

In the kitchen, Trent's mother is smoking a cigarette and finishing a Tab before she goes off to some fashion show in Century City. Trent takes a pitcher of orange juice out of the refrigerator and pours himself a glass, asks if I want one. I tell him no. He looks at his mother and takes a swallow. No one says anything for something like two minutes, not until Trent's mother says, 'Goodbye.'

Trent doesn't say anything except, 'Do you want to go to The Roxy tonight or what, Clay?'

'I don't think so,' I tell him, wondering what his mother wanted.

'Yeah? You don't.'

'I think I'm going to Daniel's party.'

'Great,' he says.

I'm about to ask him if he wants to go to a movie, but the phone rings from upstairs and Trent runs out of the kitchen to answer it. I walk back to the living room and stare out the window and watch as Trent's mother gets into her car and drives off. The maid from El Salvador stands up and slowly walks to the bathroom and I can hear her laughing, then retching and then laughing again. Trent comes into the living room looking pissed off and sits in front of the TV; phone call probably wasn't too good.

'I think your maid is sick or something,' I mention.

Trent looks over at the bathroom and says, 'Is she freaking out again?'

I sit on another couch. 'I guess.'

'Mom's going to fire her soon enough.' He takes a swallow of the orange juice he's still holding and stares at MTV.

I stare out the window.

'I don't want to do anything,' he finally says.

I decide that I don't want to go to the movies either and I wonder who I should go with to Daniel's party. Maybe Blair.

'Wanna watch *Alien*?' Trent asks, eyes closed, feet on

the glass coffee table. 'Now that would freak her out completely.'

I decide to bring Blair to Daniel's party. I drive to her house in Beverly Hills and she's wearing a pink hat and a blue miniskirt and yellow gloves and sunglasses and she tells me that at Fred Segal today someone told her that she should be in a band. And she mentions something about starting one, maybe something a little New Wave. I smile and say that sounds like a good idea, not sure if she's being sarcastic, and I grip the steering wheel a little tighter.

I hardly know anyone at the party and I finally find Daniel sitting, drunk and alone, by the pool, wearing black jeans and a white Specials T-shirt and sunglasses. I sit down next to him while Blair gets us drinks. I'm not sure if Daniel's staring into the water or if he's just passed out, but he finally speaks up and says, 'Hello, Clay.'

'Hi, Daniel.'

'Having a good time?' he asks real slowly, turning to face me.

'I just got here.'

'Oh.' He pauses for a minute. 'Who'd you come with?'

'Blair. She's getting a drink.' I take off my sunglasses and look at his bandaged hand. 'I think she thinks that we're lovers.'

Daniel leaves his sunglasses on and nods and doesn't smile.

I put my sunglasses back on.

Daniel turns back to the pool.

'Where are your parents?' I ask.

'My parents?'

'Yeah.'

'In Japan, I think.'

'What are they doing there?'

'Shopping.'

I nod.

'They might be in Aspen,' he says. 'Does it make any difference?'

Blair comes over with a gin and tonic in one hand and a beer in the other and she hands me the beer and lights a cigarette and says, 'Don't talk to that guy in the blue and red Polo shirt. He's a total narc,' and then, 'Are my sunglasses crooked?'

'No,' I tell her, and she smiles and then puts her hand on my leg and whispers into my ear, 'I don't know anyone here. Let's leave. Now.' She glances over at Daniel. 'Is he alive?'

'I don't know.'

'What?' Daniel turns to look at us. 'Hi, Blair.'

'Hi, Daniel,' Blair says.

'We're leaving,' I tell him, kind of excited by Blair's whisper and the gloved hand on my thigh.

'Why?'

'Why? Well, because . . .' My voice trails off.

'But you just got here.'

'But we really have to go.' I don't want to stay that much either and maybe going over to Blair's house seems like a good idea.

'Stick around.' Daniel tries to lift himself from the chaise longue but can't.

'Why?' I ask.

This confuses him, I guess, because he doesn't say anything.

Blair looks over at me.

'Just to be here,' he says.

'Blair isn't feeling well,' I tell him.

'But I wanted you to meet Carleton and Cecil. They were supposed to be here but their limo broke down in the Palisades and . . .' Daniel sighs and looks back into the pool.

'Sorry, dude,' I say, getting up. 'We'll have lunch.'

'Carleton goes to A.F.I.'

'Well, Blair really doesn't . . . She wants to go. Now.'

Blair nods her head and coughs.

'Maybe I'll drop by later,' I tell him, feeling guilty about leaving so soon; feeling guilty about going to Blair's house.

'No, you won't.' Daniel sits back down and sighs again.

Blair's getting really anxious and says to me, 'Listen, I'm really not too crazy about arguing over this all fucking night. Let's go, Clay.' She finishes the rest of the gin and tonic.

'See, Daniel, we're leaving, okay?' I say. 'Bye.'

Daniel tells me that he'll call me tomorrow. 'Let's have lunch or something.'

'Great,' I say, without a whole lot of enthusiasm. 'Lunch.'

Once in the car, Blair says, 'Let's go somewhere. Hurry.'

I'm thinking to myself, Why don't you just say it? 'Where?' I ask.

She stalls, names a club.

'I left my wallet at home,' I lie.

'I have a pass there,' she says, knowing I lied.

'I really don't want to.'

She turns the volume on the radio up and hums along with the song for a minute and I'm thinking that I should just drive to her house. I keep driving, not sure where to go. We stop at a coffee shop in Beverly Hills and afterwards, when we get back in the car, I ask, 'Where do you want to go, Blair?'

'I want to go . . .' she stops. 'To my house.'

I'm lying in Blair's bed. There are all these stuffed animals on the floor and at the foot of the bed and when I roll over onto my back, I feel something hard and covered with fur and I reach under myself and it's this stuffed black cat. I drop it on the floor and then get up and take a shower. After I've toweled my hair dry, I wrap the towel around my waist and walk back into her room, start to dress. Blair's smoking a cigarette and watching MTV, the sound turned down low.

'Will you call me before Christmas?' she asks.

'Maybe.' I pull on my vest, wondering why I even came here in the first place.

'You've still got my number, don't you?' She reaches for a pad and begins to write it down.

'Yeah, Blair. I've got your number. I'll get in touch.'

I button up my jeans and turn to leave.

'Clay?'

'Yeah, Blair.'

'If I don't see you before Christmas,' she stops. 'Have a good one.'

I look at her a moment. 'Hey, you too.'

She picks up the stuffed black cat and strokes its head.

I step out the door and start to close it.

'Clay?' she whispers loudly.

I stop but don't turn around. 'Yeah?'

'Nothing.'

It hadn't rained in the city for too long and Blair would keep calling me up and tell me that the two of us should get together and go to the beach club. I'd be too tired or stoned or wasted to get up in the afternoon to even go out and sit beneath the umbrellas in the hot sun at the beach club with Blair. So the two of us decided to go to Pajaro Dunes in Monterey where it was cool and where the sea was shimmering and green and my parents had a house on the beach. We drove up in my car and we slept in the master bedroom, and we drove into town and bought food and cigarettes and candles. There was nothing much to do in town; an old movie theater in need of paint and seagulls and crumbling docks and Mexican fishermen who whistled at Blair and an old church Blair took pictures of but didn't go in. We found a case of champagne in the garage and drank the whole case that week. We'd open a bottle usually in the late morning after we went walking along the beach. In the early morning we'd make love, either in the living room, or, if not in the living room, then on the floor in the master bedroom, and we'd close the blinds and light the candles we'd bought in town and we'd watch our shadows, illuminated against the white walls, move, shift.

The house was old and faded and had a courtyard and a tennis court, but we didn't play tennis. Instead, I'd wander around the house at night and listen to old records I used to like and sit in the courtyard and drink what was left of the champagne. I didn't like the house that much, and sometimes I'd have to go out onto the deck at night because I couldn't stand the white walls and the thin venetian blinds and the black tile in the kitchen. I'd walk along the beach at night and sometimes sit down in the damp sand and smoke a cigarette and stare up at the lighted house and see Blair's silhouette in the living room, talking on the phone to someone who was in Palm Springs. When I came back in we'd both be drunk and she would suggest that we go swimming, but it was too cold and dark, and so we'd sit in the small jacuzzi in the middle of the courtyard and make love.

During the day I'd sit in the living room and try to read the San Francisco Chronicle and she'd walk along the beach and collect seashells, and before too long we started going to bed sometime before dawn and then waking up in *the midafternoon, and then we'd open another bottle. One day we took the convertible and drove to a secluded part of the beach. We ate caviar and Blair had chopped up some onions and eggs and cheese, and we brought fruit and these cinnamon cookies Blair was really into, and a six-pack of Tab, because that and the champagne were all Blair would drink, and we'd either jog on the empty shore or try to swim in the rough surf.*

But I soon became disoriented and I knew I'd drunk too much, and whenever Blair would say something, I found myself closing my eyes and sighing. The water turned colder, raging, and the sand became wet, and Blair would sit by herself on the deck overlooking the sea and spot boats in the afternoon fog. I'd watch her play Solitaire through the glass window in the living room, and I'd hear the boats moan and creak, and Blair would pour herself another glass of champagne and it would all unsettle me.

Soon the champagne ran out and I opened the liquor cabinet. Blair got tan and so did I, and by the end of the week, all we did was watch television, even though the reception wasn't too good, and drink bourbon, and Blair would arrange shells into circular patterns on the floor of the living room. When Blair muttered one night, while we sat on opposite sides of the living room, 'We should have gone to Palm Springs,' I knew then that it was time to leave.

After leaving Blair I drive down Wilshire and then onto Santa Monica and then I drive onto Sunset and take

Beverly Glen to Mulholland, and then Mulholland to Sepulveda and then Sepulveda to Ventura and then I drive through Sherman Oaks to Encino and then into Tarzana and then Woodland Hills. I stop at a Sambo's that's open all night and sit alone in a large empty booth and the winds have started and they're blowing so hard that the windows are shaking and the sounds of them trembling, about to break, fill the coffee shop. There are these two young guys in the booth next to mine, both wearing black suits and sunglasses and the one with a Billy Idol button pinned to his lapel keeps hitting his hand against the table, like he's trying to keep beat. But his hand's shaking and his rhythm's off and every so often his hand falls off the table and hits nothing. The waitress comes over to their table and hands them the check and says thank you and the one with the Billy Idol pin grabs the check away from her and looks it over, fast.

'Oh, for Christ's sake, can't you add?'

'I think it's right,' the waitress says, a little nervously.

'Oh yeah, do you?' he sneers.

I get the feeling something bad's going to happen, but the other one says, 'Forget it,' and then, 'Jesus, I hate the fucking Valley,' and he digs into his pocket and throws a ten on the table.

His friend gets up, belches, and mutters, 'Fucking Valleyites,' loudly enough for her to hear. 'Go spend the rest of it at the Galleria, or wherever the hell you go to,' and then they walk out of the restaurant and into the wind.

When the waitress comes to my table to take my order

she seems really shaken up. 'Pill-popping bastards. I been to other places outside the Valley and they aren't all that great,' she tells me.

I stop at a newsstand on the way back home and buy some porno magazine with two girls holding riding crops in a laminated photo on the cover. I stand really still and the streets are empty and it's quiet and I can only hear the sound of the papers and magazines rustling, the newsstand guy running around putting bricks on top of the stacks so they don't blow away. I can also hear the sound of coyotes howling and dogs barking and palm trees shaking in the wind up in the hills. I get into my car and the wind rocks it for a minute and then I drive away, up toward my house, in the hills.

From my bed, later that night, I can hear the windows throughout the house rattling, and I get really freaked out and keep thinking that they're going to crack and shatter. It wakes me up and I sit up in bed and look over at the window and then glance over at the Elvis poster, and his eyes are looking out the window, beyond, into the night, and his face looks almost alarmed at what it might be seeing, the word 'Trust' above the worried face. And I think about the billboard on Sunset and the way Julian looked past me at Cafe Casino, and when I finally fall asleep, it's Christmas Eve.

Daniel calls me on the day before Christmas and tells me that he's feeling better and that last night, at his party, someone slipped him a bad Quaalude. Daniel also thinks that Vanden, a girl he saw at school in New Hampshire, is pregnant. He remembers that at some party before he left, she had mentioned something about it, half-jokingly. And Daniel got this letter from her a couple of days ago and he tells me that Vanden might not be coming back; that she might be starting a punk-rock group in New York called The Spider's Web; that she might be living with this drummer from school in the Village; that they might get a gig to open for someone at the Peppermint Lounge or CBGB's; that she might or might not be coming out to L.A.; that it might or might not be Daniel's kid; that she might or might not get an abortion, get rid of it; that her parents have divorced and her mother moved back to Connecticut and that she might or might not go back there and stay with her for a month or so, and her father, some big shot at ABC, is worried about her. He says that the letter wasn't too clear.

I'm lying on my bed, watching MTV, the phone cradled in my neck, and I tell him not to worry and then ask him if his parents are coming back for Christmas and he says that they'll be gone another two weeks and that he's going to spend Christmas with some friends in Bel Air. He was going to spend it with a girl he knows in Malibu, but she has mono and he doesn't think that it would be such a hot idea and I agree with him and Daniel asks if he should get in touch with Vanden and I'm surprised at how much strength it takes to care enough to urge him to do so and he says that he doesn't see the point and says Merry Christmas dude and we hang up.

I'm sitting in the main room at Chasen's with my parents and sisters and it's late, nine-thirty or ten, on Christmas Eve. Instead of eating anything, I look down at my plate and move the fork across it, back and forth, and become totally fixated on the fork cutting a path between the peas. My father startles me by pouring some more champagne into my glass. My sisters look bored and tan and talk about anorexic friends and some Calvin Klein model and they look older than I remember them looking, even more so when they hold their glasses up by the stem and drink the champagne slowly; they tell me a couple of jokes that I don't get and tell my father what they want for Christmas.

We picked my father up earlier tonight at his penthouse in Century City. It seemed that he had already opened a bottle of champagne and had drunk most of it before we arrived. My father's penthouse in Century City, the penthouse he moved into after my parents separated, is pretty big and nicely decorated and has a large jacuzzi outside the bedroom that's always warm and steaming. He and my mother, who haven't said that much to each other since the separation, which was, I think, about a year ago, seemed really nervous and irritated by the fact that the holidays have to bring them together, and they sat across from each other in the living room and said, I think, only four words to each other.

'Your car?' my father asked.

'Yes,' my mother said, looking over at the small Christmas tree that his maid decorated.

'Fine.'

Dad finishes his glass of champagne and pours himself another. Mother asks for the bread. My father wipes his mouth with his napkin, clears his throat and I tense up, knowing that he's going to ask everybody what they want for Christmas, even though my sisters have already told him. My father opens his mouth. I shut my eyes and he asks if anyone would like dessert. Definite anticlimax. The waiter comes over. I tell him no. I don't look at my parents too much, just keep running my hand through my hair, wishing I had some coke, anything, to get through this and I look around the restaurant, which is only half-full; people are murmuring to each other and their whispers carry somehow and I realize that all it comes down to is that I'm this eighteen-year-old boy with shaking hands and blond hair and with the beginnings of a tan and semistoned sitting in Chasen's on Doheny and Beverly, waiting for my father to ask me what I want for Christmas.

No one talks about anything much and no one seems to mind, at least I don't. My father mentions that one of his business associates died of pancreatic cancer recently and my mother mentions that someone she knows, a tennis partner, had a mastectomy. My father orders another bottle – third? fourth? – and mentions another deal. The older of my two sisters yawns, picks at her salad. I think about Blair alone in her bed stroking that stupid black cat and the billboard that says, 'Disappear Here' and

Julian's eyes and wonder if he's for sale and people are afraid to merge and the way the pool at night looks, the lighted water, glowing in the backyard.

Jared walks in, not with Blair's father, but with a famous model who doesn't take off her fur coat and Jared doesn't take off his dark glasses. Another man my father knows, some guy from Warner Brothers, comes over to the table and wishes us a Merry Christmas. I don't listen to the conversation. Instead I look over at my mother, who stares into her glass and one of my sisters tells her a joke and she doesn't get it and orders a drink. I wonder if Blair's father knows that Jared is at Chasen's tonight with this famous model. I hope I'll never have to do this again.

We leave Chasen's and the streets are empty and the air's still dry and hot and the wind's still blowing. On Little Santa Monica, a car lays overturned, its windows broken, and as we pass it, my sisters crane their necks to get a closer look and they ask my mother, who's driving, to slow down and she doesn't and my sisters complain. We drive to Jimmy's and my mother brings the Mercedes to a stop and we get out and the valet takes it and we all sit on a couch next to a small table in the darkened bar area. Jimmy's is pretty empty; except for a few scattered couples at the bar and another family that sits across from us, there's nobody in the bar. A piano player's singing 'September Song' and he sings softly. My father complains that he should be playing Christmas carols. My sisters go to the restroom and when they come back they tell us that they saw a lizard in one of the stalls and my mother says she doesn't get it.

I start to flirt with the oldest girl from the family across from us and I wonder if our family looks like this one does. The girl looks a lot like a girl I was seeing for a little while in New Hampshire. She has short blond hair and blue eyes and a tan and when she notices me staring at her, she looks away, smiling. My father requests a phone, and a phone with a long extension cord is brought over to the couch and my father calls his father up in Palm Springs and we all wish him a Merry Christmas and I feel like a fool saying, 'Merry Christmas, Grandpa,' in front of this girl.

On the way home, after dropping my father off at his penthouse in Century City, I keep my face pressed against the window of the car and stare out at the lights of the Valley, drifting up toward the hills as we drive onto Mulholland. One of my sisters has put my mother's fur coat on and has fallen asleep. The gate opens and the car enters the driveway. My mother presses a button that closes the gate and I try to wish her a Merry Christmas, but the words just don't come out and I leave her sitting in the car.

Christmas in Palm Springs. It was always hot. Even if it was raining, it was still hot. Christmas, last Christmas, after it was all over, after the old house was left, it got hotter than a lot of people could remember. No one wanted to believe that it could get as hot as it had become; it was simply impossible. But the temperature readings at the Security National Bank in Rancho Mirage would read 111 and 112 and 115 and all I could do was stare at the numbers, refusing to believe that it could get that hot, that hellish. But then I'd look across the desert and a hot wind would whip into my face and the sun would glare down so hard that my sunglasses couldn't keep the shine away and I'd have to squint to see that the metal grids in the crosswalk signs were twisting, writhing, actually melting in the heat, and I knew that I had to believe it.

The nights during Christmas weren't any better. It would still be light at seven and the sky would stay orange until eight and the hot winds would come through the canyons and filter out over the desert. When it got really dark the nights would be black and hot and on some nights these weird white clouds would drift slowly through the sky and disappear by dawn. It would also be quiet. It was strange to drive down 110 at one or two in the morning. There wouldn't be any cars out, and if I stopped by the side of the road and turned the radio off and rolled down the windows, I couldn't hear anything. Only my own breath, which was all raspy and dry and came in uneven gasps. But I wouldn't do this for long, because I'd catch a glimpse of my eyes in the rearview mirror, sockets red, scared, and I'd get really frightened for some reason and drive home quickly.

Early evenings were about the only time I'd go outside. I'd spend this time by the pool, eating banana popsicles and reading the Herald Examiner, *when there was some shade in the backyard, and the pool would be totally still except for an occasional ripple caused by big yellow and black bees with huge wings and black dragonflies, crashing into the pool, driven mad by the insane heat.*

Last Christmas in Palm Springs, I'd be lying in bed, naked, and even with the air conditioner on, the cool air blowing over me and a bowl of ice, some of it wrapped in a towel, next to the bed, I couldn't become cool. Visions of driving through town and feeling the hot winds on my shoulder and watching the heat rise up out of the desert would make me feel warm and I'd force myself up and walk downstairs out onto the deck by the lighted pool in the middle of the night and I'd try to smoke a joint but I could barely breathe. I'd smoke it anyway, just to get to sleep. I could only stay outside for so long. There'd be these strange sounds and lights next door, and I'd go back upstairs to my room and lock the door and finally fall asleep.

When I woke up in the afternoon, I'd come downstairs and my grandfather would tell me that he heard strange things at night and when I asked him what strange things, he said that he couldn't put his finger on it and so he'd shrug and finally say that it must have been his imagination, probably nothing. The dog would bark all night and when I'd wake up to tell it to be quiet, it would look freaked out, its eyes wide, panting, shaking, but I'd never go outside to see why the dog was barking and I'd lock myself back in my room and put the towel, damp, cool, over my eyes. The next day, out by the pool, there was an empty package of cigarettes. Lucky Strikes. No one smokes cigarettes in the family. The next day my father had new locks put on all the doors and the gates in back, while my mother and sisters took the Christmas tree down, while I slept.

A couple hours later, Blair calls. She tells me there's a picture of her father and her at a premiere in the new *People*. She also says that she's drunk and in the house alone and that her family is down the street at someone's screening room, watching a rough cut of her father's new film. She also tells me that she's nude and in bed and that she misses me. I start to walk around the room, nervous, while I listen to her. Then I stare at myself in the mirror in my closet. I spot this small shoebox in the corner of the closet and look through it while I'm on the phone with Blair. There are all these photographs in the box: a picture of Blair and me at Prom; one of us at Disneyland on Grad Nite; a couple of us at the beach in Monterey; and couple of others from a party in Palm Springs; a picture of Blair in Westwood I had taken one day when the two of us had left school early, with Blair's initials on the back of the photo. I also find this picture of myself, wearing jeans and no shirt and no shoes, lying on the floor, with sunglasses on, my hair wet, and I think about who took it and can't remember. I smooth it out and try to look at myself. I think about it some more and then put it away. There are other photographs in the box but I can't deal with looking at them, at old snapshots of Blair and me and so I put the shoebox back in the closet.

Light a cigarette and turn on MTV and turn off the

sound. An hour passes, Blair keeps talking, tells me that she still likes me and that we should get together again and that just because we haven't seen each other for four months is no reason to break up. I tell her we have been together, I mention last night. She says you know what I mean and I start to dread sitting in the room, listening to her talk. I look over at the clock. It's almost three. I tell her I can't remember what our relationship was like and I try to steer the conversation away to other topics, about movies or concerts or what she's been doing all day, or what I've been doing tonight. When I get off the phone with her, it's almost dawn, Christmas Day.

It's Christmas morning and I'm high on coke, and one of my sisters has given me this pretty expensive leather-bound datebook, the pages are big and white and the dates elegantly printed on top of them, in gold and silver lettering. I thank her and kiss her and all that and she smiles and pours herself another glass of champagne. I tried to keep a datebook one summer, but it didn't work out. I'd get confused and write down things just to write them down and I came to this realization that I didn't do enough things to keep a datebook. I know that I won't use this one and I'll probably take it back to New Hampshire with me and it'll just lie on my desk for three or four months, unused, blank. My mother watches us, sitting on the edge of the couch in the living room, sipping champagne. My sisters open their gifts casually, indifferent. My father looks neat and hard and is writing out checks for my sisters and me and I wonder why he couldn't have written them out before, but I forget about it and look out the window; at the hot wind blowing through the yard. The water in the pool ripples.

It's a really sunny, warm Friday after Christmas and I decide I need to work on my tan so I go with a bunch of people, Blair and Alana and Kim and Rip and Griffin, to the beach club. I get to the club before anyone else does and while the attendant parks my car, I sit on a bench and wait for them, staring out at the expanse of sand that meets the water, where the land ends. Disappear here. I stare out at the ocean until Griffin drives up in his Porsche. Griffin knows the parking attendant and they talk for a couple of minutes. Rip drives up soon after in his new Mercedes and also seems to know the attendant and when I introduce Rip to Griffin they laugh and tell me that they know each other and I wonder if they've slept together and I get really dizzy and have to sit down on the bench. Alana and Kim and Blair drive up in someone's convertible Cadillac.

'We just had lunch at the country club,' Blair says, turning the radio down. 'Kim got lost.'

'I did not,' Kim says.

'So she didn't believe I remembered where it was and we had to stop at this gas station to ask for directions and Kim asks this guy who works there for his phone number.'

'He was gorgeous,' Kim exclaims.

'So what? He pumps gas,' Blair shrieks, getting out of the car, looking great in a one-piece. 'Are you ready for this? His name is Moose.'

'I don't care what his name is. He is totally gorgeous,' Kim says again.

On the beach, Griffin has smuggled rum and Coke in and we're drinking what's left of it. Rip practically takes his bathing suit off so his tan line'll be exposed. I don't put enough tanning oil on my legs or chest. Alana has brought a portable tape-deck and keeps playing the same INXS song, over and over; talk of the new Psychedelic Furs album goes around; Blair tells everyone that Muriel just got out of Cedars-Sinai; Alana mentions that she called Julian up to ask him if he wanted to come but there wasn't anyone home. Everyone eventually stops talking and concentrates on what sun is left. Some Blondie song comes on and Blair and Kim ask Alana to turn it up. Griffin and I get up to go to the locker room. Deborah Harry is asking, 'Where is my wave?'

'What's wrong?' Griffin asks, staring at himself in the mirror once we're in the men's room.

'I'm just tense,' I tell him, splashing water on my face.

'Things'll be okay,' Griffin says.

And there, back on the beach, in the sun, staring out into the Pacific, it seems really possible to believe Griffin. But I get sunburned and when I stop at Gelson's for some cigarettes and a bottle of Perrier, I find a lizard in the front seat. The checkout clerk is talking about murder statistics and he looks at me for some reason and asks if I'm feeling okay. I don't say anything, just walk quickly out of the market. When I get home, I take a shower, turn on the stereo and that night I can't get to sleep; the sunburn's uncomfortable, and MTV's giving me a headache and I take some Nembutal Griffin slipped me in the parking lot at the beach club.

I get up late the next morning to the blare of Duran Duran coming from my mother's room. The door's open and my sisters are lying on the large bed, wearing bathing suits, leafing through old issues of *GQ*, watching some porno film on the Betamax with the sound turned off. I sit down on the bed, also in my bathing suit, and they tell me that Mom went out to lunch and that the maid went shopping and I watch about ten minutes of the movie, wondering whose it is – my mom's? sisters'? Christmas present from a friend? the person with the Ferrari? mine? One of my sisters says that she hates it when they show the guy coming and I walk downstairs, out to the pool, do my laps.

When I was fifteen and first learned how to drive, in Palm Springs, I'd take my father's car while my parents were asleep and my sisters and I would drive around the desert, in the middle of the night, Fleetwood Mac or Eagles on, loud, top down, hot winds blowing, making the palm trees bend, silent. And one night my sisters and I took the car out and it was a night where there wasn't any moon and the wind was strong, and someone had just dropped me off from a party that hadn't been too fun. The McDonald's we were going to stop at was closed due to some power outage caused by the winds and I was tired and my sisters were fighting and I was on the way back home when I saw what I thought was a bonfire from about a mile down the highway, but as I drove closer I saw that it wasn't a bonfire but a Toyota parked at this strange, crooked angle, its hood open, flames pouring out of the engine. The front windshield was smashed open and a Mexican woman was sitting on the curb, on the side of the highway, crying. There were two or three kids, Mexican also, standing behind her, staring at the fire, gaping at the rising flames, and I was wondering why there were no other cars out to stop or help. My sisters stopped fighting and told me to stop the car so that they could watch. I had an urge to stop, but I didn't. I slowed down, and then drove quickly away and pushed back in the tape my sisters had taken out when they first saw the flames, and turned it up, loud, and drove through every red light until I got back to our house.

I don't know why the fire bothered me, but it did, and I had these visions of a child, not yet dead, lying across the flames, burning. Maybe some kid, thrown through the windshield and who'd fallen onto the engine, and I asked my sisters if they thought they saw a kid burning, melting, on the engine and they said no, did you?, neato, and I checked the papers the next day to make sure there hadn't been one. And later that same night I sat out by the pool, thinking about it until I finally fell asleep, but not before *the power went out due to the wind and the pool went black.*

And I remember that at that time I started collecting all these newspaper clippings; one about some twelve-year-old kid who accidentally shot his brother in Chino; another about a guy in Indio who nailed his kid to a wall, or a door, I can't remember, and then shot him, point-blank in the face, and one about a fire at a home for the elderly that killed twenty and one about a housewife who while driving her children home from school flew off this eighty-foot embankment near San Diego, instantly killing herself and the three kids and one about a man who calmly and purposefully ran over his ex-wife somewhere near Reno, paralyzing her below the neck. I collected a lot of clippings during that time because, I guess, there were a lot to be collected.

It's a Saturday night and on some Saturday nights when there's not a party to go to and no concerts around town and everyone's seen all the movies, most people stay at home and invite friends over and talk on the phone. Sometimes someone will drop by and talk and have a drink and then get back into his car and drive over to somebody else's house. On some Saturday nights there'll be three or four people who drive from one house to another. Who drive from about ten on Saturday night until just before dawn the next morning. Trent stops by and tells me about how 'a couple of hysterical J.A.P.s' in Bel Air have seen what they called some kind of monster, talk of a werewolf. One of their friends has supposedly disappeared. There's a search party in Bel Air tonight and they've found nothing except – and now Trent grins – the body of a mutilated dog. The 'J.A.P.s', who Trent says are 'really out of their heads,' went to spend the night at a friend's house in Encino. Trent says that the J.A.P.s probably drank too much Tab, had some kind of allergic reaction. Maybe, I say, but the story makes me uneasy. After Trent leaves I try to call Julian, but there's no answer and I wonder where he could be and after I hang the phone up, I'm pretty sure I can hear someone screaming in the house next to us, down the canyon, and I close my window. I can also hear the dog barking out in back and KROQ is playing old Doors songs and *War of the Worlds* is on channel thirteen and I switch it to some religious program where this preacher is yelling 'Let God use you. God wants to use you. Lie back and let him use you, use you.' 'Lie back,' he keeps chanting. 'Use you, use you.' I'm drinking gin and melted ice in bed and imagine that I can hear someone breaking in. But Daniel says, over the phone, that it's probably my sisters getting something to drink. It's hard to believe Daniel tonight; on the news I hear there were four people beaten to death in the hills last night and I stay up most of the night, looking out the window, staring into the backyard, looking for werewolves.

At Kim's new house, in the hills overlooking Sunset, the gates are open but there don't seem to be too many cars around. After Blair and I walk up to the door and ring the doorbell, it takes a long time for anybody to open it. Kim finally does, wearing tight faded jeans, high black leather boots, white T-shirt, smoking a joint. She takes a hit off it before hugging both of us and saying 'Happy New Year,' then leads us into a high-ceilinged entrance room and tells us she just moved in three days ago and that 'Mom's in England with Milo' and that they haven't had time to furnish it yet. But the floors are carpeted, she tells us, and says that it's a good thing and I don't ask her why she thinks it's a good thing. She tells us that the house is pretty old, that the guy who owned it before was a Nazi. On the patios, there are these huge pots holding small trees with swastikas painted on them. 'They're called Nazi pots,' Kim says.

We follow her downstairs to where there are only about twelve or thirteen people. Kim tells us that Fear's supposed to play tonight. She introduces Blair and me to Spit, who's a friend of the drummer's, and Spit has really pale skin, paler than Muriel's, and short greasy hair and a skull earring and dark circles under his eyes, but Spit's mad and after saying hi, tells Kim that she has to do something about Muriel.

'Why?' Kim asks, inhaling on the joint.

'Because the bitch said I looked dead,' Spit says, eyes wide.

'Oh, Spit,' Kim says.

'She says that I smell like a dead animal.'

'Come on, Spit, forget it,' Kim says.

'You know I don't keep dead animals in my room

anymore.' He looks over at Muriel, who's at the end of the long bar, laughing, holding a glass of punch.

'Oh, she's wonderful, Spit,' Kim says. 'She's just been taking sixty milligrams of lithium a day. She's just tired.' Kim turns to Blair and me. 'Her mother just bought her a fifty-five-thousand-dollar Porsche.' Then she looks back at Spit. 'Can you believe it?'

Spit says he can't and that he's going to try to forget about it and decide what albums to play and Kim tells him, 'Go ahead,' and then before he goes over to the stereo, 'Listen, Spit, don't get Muriel down. Just keep quiet. She just left Cedars-Sinai and once she gets drunk, she's fine. She's just a little strung out.'

Spit ignores this and holds up an old Oingo Boingo record.

'Can I play this or not?'

'Why don't you save that for later?'

'Listen, Kim-ber-ly, I'm getting bored,' he says, teeth gritted.

Kim pulls a joint out of her back pocket and hands it to him.

'Just cool it, Spit.'

Spit says thanks and then sits down on the couch next to the fireplace, with the huge replica of the American flag draped over it, and stares at the joint a long time before he lights it.

'Well, you two look fabulous,' Kim says.

'So do you,' Blair tells her. I nod. I'm tired and a little stoned and didn't really want to come, but Blair actually came over to my house earlier and we went swimming and then to bed and Kim called up.

'Is Alana coming?' Blair asks.

'No, can't make it.' Kim shakes her head, taking another hit off the joint. 'Going to the Springs.'

'What about Julian?' Blair asks.

'Nope. Too busy fucking Beverly Hills lawyers for money,' Kim sighs, then laughs.

I'm about to ask her what she meant by that when suddenly someone calls out her name and Kim says, 'Oh, shit, the liquor guy just arrived' and walks off and I look out past the big lighted pool, out over Hollywood; blanket of lights under a neon purple sky and Blair asks me if I'm okay and I say sure.

Some young guy, eighteen or nineteen, brings in a large cardboard box and sets it on the bar and Kim signs something and tips him and he says, 'Happy New Year, dudes' and leaves. Kim takes a bottle of champagne out of the box, opens it expertly and calls out, 'Everybody take a bottle. It's Perrier-Jouet. It's chilled.'

'You convinced me, you rat.' Muriel runs over and hugs Kim and Kim gives her a bottle.

'Is Spit pissed at me or something? All I said was that he looked dead,' Muriel says, opening her bottle. 'Hiya, Blair, hi, Clay.'

'He's just on edge,' Kim says. 'Wind's weird or something.'

'He's such a moron. He tells me that, "Well, I used to do well in school before they kicked me out." Huh? What in the fuck does that mean?' Muriel asks. 'Besides, the idiot uses a blowtorch to freebase.'

Kim shrugs and takes another swallow.

'Muriel, you look wonderful,' Blair says.

'Oh, Blair, you look gorgeous, as usual,' Muriel says, taking a swallow. 'And oh my God, Clay, you must give me that vest.'

I look down while opening my bottle. The vest is just a gray-and-white argyle, one of the triangles dark red.

'It looks as if you got stabbed or something. Please let me wear it,' Muriel pleads, touching the vest.

I smile and look at her and then realize that she's totally serious and I'm too tired to say no so I pull it off and hand it to her and she puts it on, laughing. 'I'll give it back, I'll give it back, don't worry.'

There's this really irritating photographer in the room and he keeps taking pictures of everybody. He'll walk up to someone and point the camera in their face and then take two or three pictures and he comes up to me and the flash blinds me for a second and I take another swallow from the champagne bottle. Kim starts to light candles all over the room and Spit puts on an X album and someone starts to pin balloons up to one of the bare walls and the balloons, only half blown up, just hang there, limply. The door that leads out to the pool and veranda is open and also has a couple of balloons pinned on it and we walk outside, over to the pool.

'What's your mom doing?' Blair asks. 'Is she going out with Tom anymore?'

'Where did you hear that? *The Inquirer?*' Kim laughs.

'No. I saw a picture of them in the *Hollywood Reporter.*'

'She's in England with Milo, I told you,' Kim says as we get closer to the lighted water. 'At least that's what I read in *Variety.*'

'How about you?' Blair asks, starting to smile. 'Who are you seeing?'

'*Moi?*' Kim laughs and then mentions some famous young actor I think we went to school with; can't remember.

'Yeah, I heard about that. Just wanted you to verify.'

'It's true.'

'He wasn't at your Christmas party,' Blair says.

'He wasn't?' Kim looks worried. 'Are you sure?'

'He wasn't,' Blair says. 'Did you see him, Clay?'

'No, I didn't see him,' I tell her, not remembering.

'That's weird,' Kim says. 'Must have been on location.'

'How is he?'

'He's nice, he's really nice.'

'What about Dimitri?'

'Oh, so what,' Kim says.

'Does he know?' Blair asks.

'Probably. I'm not sure.'

'Do you think he's upset?'

'Listen, Jeff is a fling. I like Dimitri.'

Dimitri's sitting on a chair by the pool playing a guitar and is really tan and has short blond hair and he just sits in the chaise longue playing these strange, eerie chords and then starts to play this one riff over and over again and Kim just looks at him and doesn't say anything. The phone rings from inside and Muriel calls out, waving her hands, 'It's for you, Kim.'

Kim walks back inside and I'm about to ask Blair if she wants to go but Spit, still smoking the joint, comes over with some surfer to Dimitri and says, 'Heston has some great acid,' and the surfer with Spit looks at Blair and winks and then she pats my ass and lights a cigarette.

'Where's Kim?' Spit asks when he doesn't get an answer from Dimitri, who just stares into the pool, strumming the guitar. He then looks over at the four of us standing around him and for a minute it looks like he's going to say something. But he doesn't, just sighs and looks back at the water.

This young actress comes in with some well-known producer, who I met once at one of Blair's father's parties, and they check out the scene and walk over to Kim, who's just gotten off the phone, and she tells them that her mother's in England with Milo and the producer says that last he heard she was in Hawaii and then they mention that maybe Thomas Noguchi might be stopping by and then the actress and the producer leave and Kim walks over to where Blair and I've stood and she tells us that it was Jeff on the phone.

'What did he say?' Blair asks.

'He's an asshole. He's down in Malibu with some surfer, some guy, and they're holed up in his house.'

'What did he want?'

'To wish me a Happy New Year.' Kim looks upset.

'Well, that's nice,' Blair says hopefully.

'He said, "Have a Happy New Year, cunt,"' she says, and lights a cigarette, the champagne bottle she holds by her side almost empty. She's about to cry or say something else when Spit comes over and says that Muriel locked herself in Kim's room and so Kim and Spit and Blair and I walk inside, upstairs, down a hallway and over to Kim's door and Kim tries to open it but it's locked.

'Muriel,' she calls out, knocking. No one answers.

Spit pounds on the door, then kicks it.

'Don't fuck the door up, Spit,' Kim says, and then yells out, 'Muriel, come out.'

I look over at Blair and she looks worried. 'Do you think she's all right?'

'I don't know,' Kim says.

'What's she on?' Spit wants to know.

'Muriel?' Kim calls out again.

Spit lights another joint, leans against the wall. The photographer comes by and takes pictures of us. The door opens slowly and Muriel stands there and looks like she's been crying. She lets Spit, Kim, Blair and the photographer and me into the room and then she closes the door and locks it.

'Are you all right?' Kim asks.

'I'm fine,' she says, wiping her face.

The room's dark except for a couple of candles in the corner and Muriel sits down in the corner next to one of the candles, next to a spoon and a syringe and a little folded piece of paper with brownish powder on it and a piece of cotton. There's already some stuff in the spoon and Muriel wads the piece of cotton up as small as possible and puts it in the spoon and sticks the needle into the cotton and then draws it into the syringe. Then she pulls up her sleeve, reaches for a belt in the darkness, finds it and wraps it around her upper arm. I spot the needle tracks, look over at Blair, who's just staring at the arm.

'What's going on here?' Kim asks. 'Muriel, what are you doing?'

Muriel doesn't say anything, just slaps her arm to find

a vein and I look at my vest and it freaks me out to see that it does look like someone got stabbed, or something.

Muriel holds the syringe and Kim whispers, 'Don't do it,' but her lips are trembling and she looks excited and I can make out the beginnings of a smile and I get the feeling that she doesn't mean it and as the needle sticks into Muriel's arm, Blair gets up and says, 'I'm leaving,' and walks out of the room. Muriel closes her eyes and the syringe slowly fills with blood.

Spit says, 'Oh, man, this is wild.'

The photographer takes a picture.

My hands shake as I light a cigarette.

Muriel begins to cry and Kim strokes her head, but Muriel keeps crying and drooling all over, looking like she's laughing really and her lipstick's smeared all over her lips and nose and her mascara's running down her cheeks.

At midnight Spit tries to light some firecrackers but only a couple go off. Kim hugs Dimitri, who doesn't seem to notice or care, and he drops his guitar by his side and stares off into the pool and eleven or twelve of us stand out by the pool and someone turns the music down so that we can hear the sounds of the city celebrating, but there's not a whole lot to hear and I keep looking into the living room, where Muriel's lying on a couch, smoking a cigarette, sunglasses on, watching MTV. All we can hear are windows breaking up in the hills and dogs beginning to howl and a balloon bursts and Spit drops a champagne bottle and the American flag that's hanging like a curtain over the fireplace moves in the hot breeze and Kim gets up and lights another joint. Blair whispers 'Happy New

Year' to me and then takes her shoes off and sticks her feet into the warm, lighted water. Fear never shows up and the party ends early.

And at home that night, sometime early that morning, I'm sitting in my room watching religious programs on cable TV because I'm tired of watching videos and there are these two guys, priests, preachers maybe, on the screen, forty, maybe forty-five, wearing business suits and ties, pink-tinted sunglasses, talking about Led Zeppelin records, saying that, if they're played backwards, they 'possess alarming passages about the devil.' One of the guys stands up and breaks the record, snaps it in half, and says, 'And believe me, as God-fearing Christians, we will not allow this!' The man then begins to talk about how he's worried that it'll harm the young people. 'And the young are the future of this country,' he screams, and then breaks another record.

'Julian wants to see you,' Rip says over the phone.

'Me?'

'Yeah.'

'Did he say what for?' I ask.

'No. He didn't have your number and he wanted it and so I gave it to him.'

'He didn't have my number?'

'That's what he said.'

'I don't think he's called me.'

'Said he needed to talk to you. Listen, I don't like to relay phone messages, dude, so be grateful.'

'Thanks.'

'He said he'll be at the Chinese Theater today at three-thirty. You could meet him there, I guess.'

'What's he doing there?' I ask.

'What do you think?'

I decide to meet Julian. I drive over to the Chinese Theater on Hollywood Boulevard and stare at the foot-prints for a little while. Except for a young couple, not from L.A., taking pictures of the footprints and this suspicious-looking Oriental guy standing by the ticket booth, there's no one around. The tan blond usher standing by the door says to me, 'Hey, I know you. Two Decembers ago at a party in Santa Monica, right?'

'I don't think so,' I tell him.

'Yeah. Kicker's party. Remember?'

I tell him I don't remember and then ask him if the concession stand's open. The usher says yeah and lets me in and I buy a Coke.

'The movie already began though,' the usher tells me.

'That's okay. I don't want to see the movie,' I tell him.

The suspicious-looking Oriental guy keeps looking at his watch, finally leaves. I finish the Coke and wait until around four. Julian doesn't show up.

I drive to Trent's house, but Trent isn't there and so I sit in his room and put a movie in the Betamax and call Blair and ask her if she wants to do something tonight, go to a club or see a movie and she says she would and I start to draw on a piece of paper that's next to the phone, recopying phone numbers on it.

'Julian wants to see you,' Blair tells me.

'Yeah. I heard. Did he say what for?'

'I don't know what he wants to see you about. He just said he has to talk to you.'

'Do you have his number?' I ask.

'No. They changed all the numbers at the house in Bel Air. I think he's probably at the house in Malibu. I'm not too sure, though . . . Does it matter? He probably doesn't want to see you *that* badly.'

'Well,' I begin, 'maybe I'll stop by the house in Bel Air.'

'Okay.'

'If you want to do anything tonight, call me, okay?' I tell her.

'Okay.'

There's a long silence and she says okay once more and hangs up.

Julian's not at the house in Bel Air, but there's a note on the door saying that he might be at some house on King's Road. Julian's not at the house on King's Road either, but some guy with braces and short platinum-blond hair and a bathing suit on lifting weights is in the backyard. He puts one of the weights down and lights a cigarette and asks me if I want a Quaalude. I ask him where Julian is. There's a girl lying by the pool on a chaise longue, blond, drunk, and she says in a really tired voice, 'Oh, Julian could be anywhere. Does he owe you money?' The girl has brought a television outside and is watching some movie about cavemen.

'No,' I tell her.

'Well, that's good. He promised to pay for a gram of coke I got him.' She shakes her head. 'Nope. He never did.' She shakes her head again, slowly, her voice thick, a bottle of gin, half-empty, by her side.

The weightlifter with the braces on asks me if I want to buy a *Temple of Doom* bootleg cassette. I tell him no and then ask him to tell Julian that I stopped by. The weightlifter nods his head like he doesn't understand and the girl asks him if he got the backstage passes to the Missing Persons concert. He says, 'Yeah, baby,' and she jumps in the pool. Some caveman gets thrown off a cliff and I split.

On the way to my car I bump into Julian. He's pale beneath the tan and doesn't look too great and I get the feeling he's going to faint, standing there, looking almost dead, but his mouth opens and he says, 'Hi, Clay.'

'Hey, Julian.'

'Wanna get stoned?'

'Not now.'

'I'm glad you came by.'

'Heard you wanted to see me.'

'Yeah.'

'What did you want? What's going on?'

Julian looks down and then up at me, squinting at the setting sun and says, 'Money.'

'What for?' I ask after a little while.

He looks at the ground, touches the back of his neck and says, 'Hey, let's go to the Galleria, okay? Come on.'

I don't want to go to the Galleria and I don't want to give Julian any money either, but it's a sunny afternoon and I don't have too much else to do and so I follow Julian into Sherman Oaks.

We're sitting at a table at the Galleria. Julian's picking at a cheeseburger, not really eating it. He takes a napkin and wipes the ketchup off with it. I'm drinking a Coke. Julian says he needs some money, some cash.

'What for?' I ask.

'Do you want some fries?'

'Could you kind of get to the point?'

'An abortion for someone.' He takes a bite out of the cheeseburger and I take the napkin covered with ketchup and put it on the table behind ours.

'An abortion?'

'Yeah.'

'For who?'

There's a long pause and Julian says, 'Some girl.'

'I would think so. But who?'

'She's living with some friends in Westwood. Look, can you let me borrow the money or not?'

I look down at the people walking around the first floor of the Galleria and wonder what would happen if I spill the Coke over the side. 'Yeah,' I finally answer. 'I guess.'

'Wow. That's great,' Julian says, relieved.

'Don't you have any money?' I ask.

Julian looks at me quickly and says, 'Um, not now. But I will and, oh, by then it'll be, like, too late, you know? And I don't want to have to sell the Porsche. I mean that would be a bummer.' He takes a long pause, fingers the cheeseburger. 'Just for some abortion?' He tries to laugh.

I tell Julian that I really doubt he'd have to sell his Porsche to pay for an abortion.

'What is it really for?' I ask him.

'What do you mean?' he says, getting really defensive. 'It's for an abortion.'

'Julian, that's a lot of money for an abortion.'

'Well, the doctor's expensive,' he says slowly, lamely. 'She doesn't want to go to one of those clinics or anything. I don't know why. She just doesn't.'

I sigh and sit back in my seat.

'I swear to God, Clay, it's for an abortion.'

'Julian, come on.'

'I have credit cards and a checking account, but I think my parents put a freeze on it. All I need is some cash. Will you give me the money or not?'

'Yeah, Julian, I will, but I just want you to tell me what it's for.'

'I told you.'

We get up and begin to walk around. Two girls pass us

and smile. Julian smiles back. We stop at some punk clothing store and Julian picks up a pair of police boots and looks at them closely.

'These are weird looking,' he says. 'I like them.'

He puts them down and then starts to bite his fingernails. He picks up a belt, a black leather one, and looks at it closely. And then I remember Julian in fifth grade playing soccer with me after school and then him and Trent and me going to Magic Mountain the next day on Julian's eleventh birthday.

'Do you remember when we were in fifth grade?' I ask him. 'In Sports Club, after school?'

'I can't remember,' Julian says.

He picks up another leather belt, puts it down and then the two of us leave the Galleria.

That afternoon, after Julian asked me for the money and told me to give it to him two days later at his house, I come home and the phone rings and it's Rip and he asks me if I've gotten in touch with Julian. I tell him no and Rip asks me if I need anything. I tell him I need a quarter ounce. He's silent for a long time and then says, 'Six hundred.' I look over at the Elvis Costello poster and then out the window and then I count to sixty. Rip hasn't said anything by the time I've finished counting.

'Okay?' I ask.

Rip says, 'Okay. Tomorrow. Maybe.'

I get up and drive to a record store and walk down the

aisles, look through the record bins, but I don't find anything I want that I don't already have. I pick up some of the new records and stare at the covers and before I realize it, an hour's passed and it's almost dark outside.

Spit walks into the record store and I almost walk over to him, say hi, ask about Kim, but I spot the track marks on his arm and I walk out of the store, wondering if Spit would remember me anyway. As I walk to my car, I see Alana and Kim and this blond rockabilly guy named Benjamin coming toward me. It's too late for me to turn around, so I smile and walk up to them and the four of us end up at some sushi bar in Studio City.

At the sushi bar in Studio City, Alana doesn't say much. She keeps looking down at her Diet Coke and lighting cigarettes and after a few drags, putting them out. When I ask her about Blair, she looks at me and says, 'Do you really want to know?' and then smiles grimly and says, 'You sound like you really care.' I turn away from her, kind of freaked out and talk to this Benjamin guy, who goes to Oakwood. It seems that his BMW was stolen and he goes on about how he finds it really lucky that he found a new BMW 320i in the same off-green his father originally bought him and he tells me, 'I mean, I can't believe I found it. Can you?'

'No. I can't,' I tell him, glancing over at Alana.

Kim feeds Benjamin a piece of sushi and then he takes a sip of sake he got with his fake I.D. and starts to talk about music. 'New Wave. Power Pop. Primitive Muzak. It's all bullshit. Rockabilly is where it's at. And I don't mean those limp-wristed Stray Cats, I mean real rockabilly. I'm going to New York in April to check the rockabilly scene out. I'm not too sure if it's happening there. It might be happening in Baltimore.'

'Yeah. Baltimore,' I say.

'Yeah, I like rockabilly too,' Kim says, wiping her hands. 'But I'm still into the Psychedelic Furs and I like that new Human League song.'

Benjamin says, 'The Human League are out. Over. Finished. You don't know what's going on, Kim.'

Kim shrugs. I wonder where Dimitri is; if Jeff is still holed up with some surfer out in Malibu.

'No, I mean, you really don't,' he goes on. 'I bet you don't even read *The Face*. You've got to.' He lights a clove cigarette. 'You've got to.'

'Why do you have to?' I ask.

Benjamin looks at me, runs his fingers over his pompadour and says, 'Otherwise you'll get bored.'

I say I guess so, then make plans with Kim to meet her later tonight at her house with Blair and then I go home and out to dinner with my mother. When I get home from that I take a long cold shower and sit on the floor of the stall and let the water hit me full on.

I drive over to Kim's house and find Blair sitting in Kim's room and she has this shopping bag from Jurgenson's over her head and when I come in, her body gets all tense and she turns around, startled, and she reaches over and turns down the stereo. 'Who is it?'

'It's me,' I tell her. 'Clay.'

She takes the bag off her head and smiles and tells me that she had the hiccups. There's a large dog at Blair's feet and I lean down and stroke the dog's head. Kim comes out of the bathroom, takes a drag off the cigarette Blair was smoking and then throws it on the floor. She turns the stereo back up, some Prince song.

'Jesus, Clay, you look like you're on acid or something,' Blair says, lighting another cigarette.

'I just had dinner with my mother,' I tell her.

The dog puts the cigarette out with its paw and then eats it.

Kim mentions something about an old boyfriend who had a really bad trip once. 'He took acid and didn't come down for six weeks. His parents sent him to Switzerland.' Kim turns to Blair, who's looking at the dog. The dog swallows the rest of the cigarette.

'Have I dressed down enough?' Kim asks us.

Blair nods and tells her to take the hat off.

'Should I?' Kim asks me, unsure.

'Sure, why not?' I sigh and sit on Kim's bed.

'Listen, it's early. Why don't we go to the movies,' Kim says, looking in the mirror, taking the hat off.

Blair gets up and says, 'That's a good idea. What's playing?'

The dog coughs and swallows again.

We drive to Westwood. The movie Kim and Blair want to see starts at ten and is about this group of young pretty sorority girls who get their throats slit and are thrown into a pool. I don't watch a lot of the movie, just the gory parts. My eyes keep wandering off the screen and over to the two green Exit signs that hang above the two doors in the back of the theater. The movie ends really suddenly and Kim and Blair stay for the credits and recognize a lot of the names. On the way out, Blair and Kim spot Lene, and Blair grabs my arm and says, 'Oh, no.'

'Turn around, turn around. Lene is here,' Kim says with this urgent voice. 'Don't tell her we saw her on MV3 today.'

'It's too late.' Blair smiles. 'Hello, Lene.'

Lene is too tan and only wearing faded jeans and this totally revealing Hard Rock Cafe T-shirt and she's with this really young blond boy who's also too tan and he's wearing sunglasses and shorts and Lene shouts, 'Oh my God. Blair. Kimmy.'

Lene and Blair hug each other and then Lene and Kim hug and pretend to kiss each other's cheek.

'This is Troy,' Lene says, introducing the young guy.

'This is Clay,' Blair says, putting her arm on my shoulder.

'Hi, Troy,' I say.

'Hi, Clay,' he says.

We shake hands, both grips kind of limp and shaky, and the girls seem pleased.

'Oh my God, Blair, Troy and I were on MV3 today! Did you watch it?' Lene asks.

'No,' says Blair, sounding disappointed, glancing at Kim for a moment.

'Did you?' Lene asks Kim. Kim shakes her head.

'Well, I couldn't see myself. Actually, I thought I saw myself once, but I wasn't too sure. Did you see me, Troy?'

Troy shakes his head, checks his nails.

'Troy was on it, but they missed me and I was dancing with Troy. Instead of getting me, they got some Valley bitch dancing next to Troy.' She pulls out a cigarette, looks for a lighter.

'Maybe they'll repeat it and you can look more closely,' Blair says, almost grinning.

'Oh yeah, for sure they'll repeat it,' Kim agrees, grinning, looking Troy over.

'Really?' Lene asks hopefully. I light her cigarette.

'They rerun everything,' Blair says. 'Everything.'

We never get to Nowhere Club. Kim gets lost and forgets the address and so we go, instead, to Barney's Beanery and sit there in silence and Kim talks about her party and I shoot some pool and when Blair orders a drink, the waitress asks for I.D. and Blair shows her a fake one and the waitress brings her a drink and Blair gives it to Kim, who drinks it down fast and tells Blair to order another one. And the two of them talk about how bad Lene looked on MV3 today.

Trent calls me the next night and tells me that he's feeling depressed and doesn't have any more coke, can't find Julian; having problems with some girl.

'We went to this party in the hills last night . . .' Trent starts and then stops.

'Yeah?' I ask, lying on my bed, staring at the TV.

'Well, I don't know, I think she's seeing someone else . . .' He stops again. 'We just don't have it together. I'm bummed out.'

There's another long pause. 'Yeah? Bummed out?' I ask.

'Let's go to a movie,' Trent says.

It takes me a little while to say anything because there's a video on cable of buildings being blown up in slow motion and in black and white.

On the way to the Beverly Center, Trent smokes a joint and mentions that this girl lives around the Beverly Center and that I look a little like her.

'Great,' I say.

'Girls are fucked. Especially this girl. She is so fucked up. On cocaine. On this drug called Preludin, on speed. Jesus.' Trent takes another drag, hands it to me, and then unrolls the window and stares at the sky.

We park and then walk through the empty, bright Beverly Center. All the stores are closed and as we walk up to the top floor, where the movies are playing, the whiteness of the floors and the ceilings and the walls is overpowering and we walk quickly through the empty mall and don't see one other person until we get to the theaters. There are a couple of people milling around the ticket booth. We buy our tickets and walk down the hall to theater thirteen and Trent and I are the only persons in it and we share another joint inside the small, hollow room.

As we walk out of the theater, ninety minutes, maybe two hours later, some girl with pink hair and roller skates slung over her shoulders comes up to Trent.

'Trent, like, oh my God. Isn't this place a scream?' the girl squeals.

'Hey, Ronnette, what are you doing here?' Trent is completely stoned; fell asleep during the second half of the movie.

'Like hanging around.'

'Hey, Ronnette, this is Clay. Clay, this is Ronnette.'

'Hi, Clay,' she says, flirting. 'Hey, you two, what flick did you see?' She opens a piece of Bazooka and pops it into her mouth.

'Um . . . number thirteen,' Trent says, groggy, eyes red and half closed.

'What was it called?' Ronnette asks.

'I forget,' Trent says, and looks over at me. I forgot too and so I just shrug.

'Hey, Trenty, I need a ride. Did you drive here?' she asks.

'No, well yeah. No, Clay did.'

'Oh, Clay, could you please give me a ride?'

'Sure.'

'Fab. Let me put these on and we'll go.'

On the way through the mall, a security guard, sitting alone on a white bench, smoking a cigarette, tells Ronnette that there's no roller skating in the Beverly Center.

'Too much,' Ronnette says, and rolls away.

The security guard just sits there and takes another drag and watches us leave.

Once in my car Ronnette tells us that she just finished

singing vocals, actually background vocals, on Bandarasta's new album.

'But I don't like Bandarasta. He's always calling me "Halloween" for some reason. I don't like to be called "Halloween." I don't like it at all.'

I don't ask who Bandarasta is; instead I ask her if she's a singer.

'Oh, you could say. I'm a hairdresser, really. See, I got mono and dropped out of Uni and just hung around. I paint, too . . . oh gosh, that reminds me. I left my art over at Devo's house. I think they want to use it in a video. Anyway . . .' She laughs and then stops and blows a bubble and snaps her gum. 'What did you ask me, I forgot.'

I notice that Trent's asleep and I jab him in the stomach.

'I'm up, dude, I'm up.' He sits up and unrolls his window.

'Cla-ay,' Ronnette says. 'What did you ask me. I forgot.'

'What do you do?' I ask, irritated, trying to stay awake.

'Oh, I cut everybody's hair at Flip. Oh, turn this song up. I love this song. They're gonna be at The Palace on Friday.'

'Trent, wake up, asshole,' I say loudly over the music.

'I'm up, dude, I'm up. Eyes are just tired.'

'Open them,' I tell him.

He opens them and looks around the car. 'Hair looks good,' he tells Ronnette.

'Did it myself. I had this dream, see, where I saw the whole world melt. I was standing on La Cienega and from there I could see the whole world and it was melting and it was just so strong and realistic like. And so I thought, Well, if this dream comes true, how can I stop it, you know?'

I'm nodding my head.

'How can I change things, you know? So I thought if I, like pierced my ear or something, like alter my physical image, dye my hair, the world wouldn't melt. So I dyed my hair and this pink lasts. I like it. It lasts. I don't think the world is gonna melt anymore.'

I'm not too reassured by her tone and I can't believe I'm actually nodding my head, but I pull up to Danny's Okie Dog on Santa Monica and she trips as she climbs out of the small backseat of the Mercedes and lies on the sidewalk and laughs as I drive away. I ask Trent where he met her. We pass the billboard on Sunset. Disappear Here. Wonder if he's for sale.

'Just around,' he says. 'Wanna joint?'

Next day I stop by Julian's house in Bel Air with the money in a green envelope. He's lying on his bed in a wet bathing suit watching MTV. It's dark in the room, the only light coming from the black and white images on the television.

'I brought the money,' I tell him.

'Great,' he says.

I move over to his bed and put down the money.

'You don't have to count it. It's all there.'

'Thanks, Clay.'

'What is it really for, Julian?'

Julian watches the video until it's over and then turns away and says, 'Why?'

'Because that's a lot of money.'

'Then why did you give it to me?' he asks, running his hand over his smooth, tan chest.

'Because you're a friend?' It comes out sounding like a question. I look down.

'Right,' Julian says, his eyes going back to the television. Another video flashes on.

Julian falls asleep.

I leave.

Rip calls me up and tells me that we should meet at La Scala Boutique, have a little lunch, a little chopped salad, discuss a little business. I drive to La Scala and find a parking space in back and sit there and listen to the rest of a song on the radio. A couple behind me in a dark-blue Jaguar think that I'm leaving, but I don't wave them on. I sit there a little longer and the couple in the Jaguar finally honk their horn and drive off. I get out of the car and walk into the restaurant and sit at the bar and order a glass of red wine. After I finish it, I order a second and by the time Rip arrives, I've had three glasses.

'Hey, babe, how's it going?'

I stare at the glass. 'Did you bring it?'

'Hey, babe.' The tone changes. 'I asked you how it's

going. Are you gonna answer me, or, like, what's the story?'

'I'm great, Rip. Just great.'

'That's terrific. That's all I wanted to hear. Finish the wine and we'll get a booth, okay?'

'Okay.'

'You look good.'

'Thanks,' I say, and finish the wine and leave a ten on the bar.

'Great tan,' he tells me as we sit down.

'Did you bring it?' I ask.

'Cool down . . .' Rip says, looking at the menu. 'It's getting hot. Real hot. Like last summer.'

'Yeah.'

An old woman, holding an umbrella, falls to her knees on the other side of the street.

'Remember last summer?' he's asking me.

'Not really.'

There are people standing over the old woman and an ambulance comes, but most of the people in La Scala don't seem to notice.

'Yeah, sure you do.'

Last summer. Things I remember about last summer. Hanging out at clubs: The Wire, Nowhere Club, Land's End, the Edge. An albino in Canter's around three in the morning. Huge green skull leering at drivers from a billboard on Sunset, hooded, holding a pyx, bony fingers beckoning. Saw a transvestite wearing a halter top in line at some movie. Saw a lot of transvestites that summer. Dinner at Morton's with Blair when she told me not to go to New Hampshire. I saw a midget get into a Corvette. Went to a Go-Go's concert with Julian. Party at Kim's on a hot Sunday afternoon. B-52s on the stereo. Gazpacho, chili from Chasen's, hamburgers, banana daiquiris, Double Rainbow ice cream. Two English boys lounging by the pool who tell me about how much they like working at Fred Segal. All the English boys I met that summer worked at Fred Segal. Thin French boy, who Blair slept with, smoking a joint, feet in the jacuzzi. Big black Rotweiller bites at the water and swims laps. Rip carries a plastic eyeball in his mouth. I keep staring past the palm trees, watching the skies.

Someone is supposed to be playing at The Palace tonight, but Blair's drunk and Kim spots Lene hanging out in front and the two of them groan and Blair turns the car around. Someone named Angel was supposed to go with us tonight, but earlier today she got caught in the drain of her jacuzzi and almost drowned. Kim says that The Garage reopened somewhere on La Brea and Blair drives to La Brea and then down La Brea and then up and then down once more and she can't find it. Blair laughs and says, 'This is ridiculous,' and pushes in some Spandau Ballet tape and turns the volume up.

'Let's just go to the fucking Edge,' Kim yells.

Blair begins to laugh and then says, 'Oh, all right.'

'What do you think, Clay? Should we go to the Edge?' Kim asks.

I'm sitting in the backseat drunk and I shrug, and when we get to the Edge, I drink two more drinks.

The DJ at the Edge tonight isn't wearing a shirt and his nipples are pierced and he wears a leather cowboy hat and between songs he keeps mumbling 'Hip-Hip-Hooray.' Kim tells me that the DJ obviously cannot decide whether he's butch or New Wave. Blair introduces me to one of her friends, Christie, who's on this new TV show on ABC. Christie is with Lindsay, who's tall and looks a lot like Matt Dillon. Lindsay and I walk upstairs to the restroom and do some coke in one of the stalls. Above the sink, on the mirror, someone's written in big black letters 'Gloom Rules.'

After we leave the restroom, Lindsay and I sit at the bar upstairs and he tells me that there's not too much going on anywhere in the city. I nod, watch the large strobe light blink off and on, flashing across the big dance floor. Lindsay lights my cigarette and begins to talk, but the music's loud and I can't hear a lot of what he's saying. Some surfer bumps into me and then smiles and asks for a light. Lindsay gives the boy a light and smiles back. Lindsay then begins to talk about how he hasn't met anyone for the past four months who's over nineteen. 'Blows your mind away, huh?' he screams, over the sound of the music.

Lindsay gets up and says that he spots his dealer and has to go talk to her. I sit at the bar alone and light another cigarette, order another drink. There's a fat girl also sitting alone at the near empty bar, trying to talk to the bartender, who, like the DJ, is also shirtless and dancing by himself, behind the bar, to the music that's pouring out of the club's sound system. The fat girl has a lot of makeup on and she's sipping a Tab with a straw and wearing purple Calvin Klein jeans and matching cowboy boots. The bartender isn't listening to her and I have this image of her, sitting alone in a room somewhere in the city, waiting for a phone to ring. The fat girl orders another Tab. From downstairs the music stops and the DJ announces that there'll be a miniskirt beach party at The Florentine Gardens in two weeks.

'It's really ... lively tonight,' the fat girl tells the bartender.

'Where?' the bartender asks.

The girl looks down, embarrassed for a moment, and pays for her drink and I can barely hear her mumble, 'Somewhere,' and she gets up and buttons the top button on her jeans and leaves the bar and sometime, later that night, I realize I'm going to be home for two more weeks.

The psychiatrist I see tells me that he has a new idea for a screenplay. Instead of listening, I sling a leg over the arm of the huge black leather chair in the posh office and light another cigarette, a clove. This guy goes on and on and after every couple of sentences he runs his fingers through his beard and looks at me. I have my sunglasses on and he isn't too sure if I'm looking at him. I am. The psychiatrist talks some more and soon it really doesn't matter what he says. He pauses and asks me if I would like to help him write it. I tell him that I'm not interested. The psychiatrist says something like, 'You know, Clay, that you and I have been talking about how you should become more active and not so passive and I think it would be a good idea if you would help me write this. At least a treatment.'

I mumble something, blow some of the clove smoke toward him and look out the window.

I park my car in front of Trent's new apartment, a few blocks from U.C.L.A. in Westwood, the apartment he lives in when he has classes. Rip answers the door since he's now Trent's dealer, since Trent hasn't been able to find Julian.

'Guess who's here?' Rip asks me.

'Who?'

'Guess.'

'Who?'

'Guess.'

'Tell me, Rip.'

'He's young, he's rich, he's available, he's Iranian.' Rip pushes me into the living room. 'Here's Atiff.'

Atiff, who I haven't seen since graduation, is sitting on the couch wearing Gucci loafers and an expensive Italian suit. He's a freshman at U.S.C. and drives a black 380 SL.

'Ah, Clay, how are you, my friend?' Atiff gets up from the couch and shakes my hand.

'Okay. How about you?'

'Oh, very good, very good. I just got back from Rome.'

Rip walks out of the living room and into Trent's room and turns MTV on and the sound up.

'Where's Trent?' I ask, wondering where the bar is.

'In the shower,' Atiff says. 'You look great. How was New Hampshire?'

'It was okay,' I say, and smile at Trent's roommate, Chris, who's sitting at the table in the kitchen, on the phone. He smiles back and gets up and starts pacing nervously around the kitchen. Atiff is talking about clubs in Venice and how he lost a piece of Louis Vuitton luggage in Florence. He lights a thin Italian cigarette. 'I got back two nights ago because I was told classes start soon. I am not sure when they do, but I hear that it is rather soon.' He pauses. 'Did you go to Sandra's party at Spago last night? No? It wasn't very good.'

I'm nodding and looking over at Chris, who gets off the phone and yells, 'Shit.'

'What is wrong?' asks Atiff.

'I had my guitar stolen and I had some Desoxyn hidden in it and I was supposed to give it to someone.'

'What do you do?' I ask Chris.

'Hang around U.C.L.A.'

'Enrolled in classes?'

'I think.'

'He also writes music,' says Trent, standing in the doorway, only wearing jeans, hair wet, toweling it dry. 'Play them some of your stuff.'

'Sure,' Chris says, shrugging.

Chris goes to the stereo and puts a tape in it. From where I'm standing I can see the jacuzzi, steaming, blue, lit, and past that a weight set and two bicycles. I sit down on the couch and look through some of the magazines spread across the table; a couple of GQs, and a few *Rolling Stones* and an issue of *Playboy* and the issue of *People* with the picture of Blair and her father in it and a copy of *Stereo Review* and *Surfer*. Flip through a *Playboy* then start to space out and stare at the framed poster for the 'Hotel California' album; at the hypnotizing blue lettering; at the shadow of the palms.

Trent mentions that someone named Larry didn't get into film school. The music comes out over the speakers and I try to listen to it, but Trent's still talking about Larry and Rip is cracking up hysterically in Trent's room. 'I mean his father's got a fucking series that's in the fucking top ten. He's got his own steadicam and U.S.C. still doesn't let him in? Things are fucked up.'

'They didn't let him in because he's a heroin addict,' Rip calls out.

'What bullshit,' Trent says.

'You didn't know that?' Rip laughs.

'What in the hell are you talking about?'

'He practically eats it raw,' Rip says, turning the volume on the television down. 'He used to be normal.'

'Oh shit, Rip,' I call out. 'What does normal mean to you?'

'No, I mean really normal.'

'Shit, I never knew that about Larry,' Atiff says.

'You're so full of shit,' Trent calls out to the bedroom.

'Oh, Trent, suck my dick,' Rip yells.

'Take it out,' Trent calls out, laughing, walking back to the bedroom. 'Hey, who made the reservations at Morton's?'

Déjà vu passes through me and I open a *GQ*, faces from my sisters' walls come back to me. The music is loud and the songs sound like they're being sung by a little girl and the drum machine is too noisy, and insistent. The little girl voices sing out, '*I don't know where to go / I don't know what to do / I don't know where to go / I don't know what to do / Tell me. Tell me . . .*'

'Did you make the reservations?' Trent calls again.

'You have any meth?' Chris calls back to Trent.

'No,' Trent calls back. 'Who made the reservations?'

'Yes, I made them,' Rip shouts. 'Now shut up.'

'Do any of you guys have any meth?' Chris asks.

'Meth?' Atiff asks.

'Look, we don't have any meth,' I tell him.

The music stops.

'You gotta hear this next song,' Trent says, pulling on a shirt.

Chris ignores him and picks up the phone in the kitchen. He dials and then asks whoever's on the other end if they have any meth. Chris pauses and hangs up, looking dejected.

'Some guy propositioned me today,' Rip is saying, walking into the living room. 'He just came up to me in Flip and offered me six hundred dollars to go to Laguna with him for the weekend.'

'I'm sure you're not the only guy he approached,' Trent says, coming out into the living room and opening the door that leads out to the jacuzzi. He bends down and feels the water. 'Chris, do you have any cigarettes?'

'Yeah, in my room, on the bed stand,' Chris says, dialing another number.

I stare back at the poster and wonder if I should do the coke I have in my pocket now, before we go to Morton's, or when we get there. Trent comes out of Chris's room and wants to know who's lying on the floor of Chris's room, sleeping.

'Oh, that's Alan, I think. He's been there for like two days.'

'Oh, that's great,' Trent says. 'Just great.'

'Just leave him alone. He has mono or something.'

'Let's just go,' Trent says.

Rip goes to the bathroom first and Atiff and I stand up. Chris hangs up the phone.

'Are you going to be here when I get back?' Trent asks him.

'No. Gotta go over to the Colony. Look for some meth.'

My dreams start out calmly. I'll be younger and walking home from school and the day will be overcast, clouds gray and white and some of them purple. Then it'll start to rain and I'll begin to run. After running through all this falling water for what seems to be a really long time, I'll suddenly trip into mud and fall flat on the ground and because the earth's so wet, I start to sink, and the mud fills my mouth and I start to swallow it and then it goes up through my nose and finally into my eyes, and I don't wake up until I'm completely underground.

It begins to rain in L.A. I read about the houses falling, slipping down the hills in the middle of the night and I stay up all night, usually wired on coke, until early morning to make sure nothing happens to our house. Then I go out into the damp, humid morning and get the paper, read the film section and try to ignore the rain.

Nothing much happens during the days it rains. One of my sisters buys a fish and puts it in the jacuzzi and the heat and chlorine kill it. I get these strange phone calls. Someone calls, usually late at night, and on my number, and when I answer the phone, the person on the other end doesn't say anything for three minutes. I keep count. Then I'll hear a sigh and the person hangs up. The street lights on Sunset get short-circuited, so a yellow light will be flashing at an intersection and then a green one will blink on for a couple of seconds, followed by the yellow and then the red and green lights will start to shine at the same time.

I get a message that Trent stopped by. He was wearing a really expensive suit, my sisters said, and driving someone else's Mercedes. 'Friend of mine's,' Trent told them. He also told them to tell me that Scott O.D.'d. I don't know who Scott is. It keeps raining. And that night, after I get three of the weird silent phone calls, I break a glass by throwing it against the wall. No one comes in to see what the sound was. Then I lie on the bed, awake, take twenty milligrams of Valium to come off the coke, but it doesn't get me to sleep. I turn MTV off and the radio on, but

KNAC won't come in so I turn the radio off and stare out across the Valley and look at the canvas of neon and fluorescent lights lying beneath the purple night sky and I stand there, nude, by the window, watching the clouds pass and then I lie on my bed and try to remember how many days I've been home and then I get up and pace the room and light another cigarette and then the phone will ring. This is how the nights are when it rains.

I'm sitting in Spago with Trent and Blair and Trent says he's positive that there were people doing cocaine at the bar and I tell him why don't you go join them and he tells me to shut up. Since we did half a gram before leaving Trent's apartment, none of us are too hungry, and we only order appetizers and one pizza and keep drinking grapefruit juice and vodka. Blair keeps smelling her wrist and humming along with the new Human league single that's playing over the stereo system. Blair asks the waiter, after he brings us our fourth round of greyhounds, if he was at the Edge the other night. He smiles and shakes his head.

'So tell me,' Blair asks Trent. 'Is Walker really an alcoholic?'

'Yeah, yeah. Walker is,' Trent says.

'I knew it. But Walker's great though. Walker's nice.'

Trent laughs and agrees, then looks at me.

I'm totally startled for a moment and I look at both of them and say, 'Walker *is* nice.' I don't know who Walker is.

'Yeah, I like Walker,' Trent says.

'Yeah, Walker's nice.' Blair nods.

'Hey, did I tell you,' Trent begins. 'I'm going to the Springs tomorrow. I have to go down and watch some dumb-ass Mexican gardener plant cactus in the backyard. Is that the most typical thing you have ever heard of? So typical. Mom asked me and I said, "No way, dude," and she said, "You never do anything for me," and I mean, she was right, and so I said, "Okay," because I felt sorry for her, you know? Besides, I heard that Sandy has some great coke and he'll be there.'

Blair smiles. 'You're such a nice boy.'

It's getting to be toward midnight and someone pays the check and I tell Trent, after Blair's left for the restroom, that I didn't have the slightest idea who Walker is. Trent looks at me and says, 'You don't make any sense, you know that?'

'I make sense.'

'No, dude. You're ridiculous.'

'Why don't I make sense?'

'Because you just don't.'

'That doesn't make sense.'

'Maybe it doesn't.'

'Jesus.'

'You're a fool, Clay,' Trent laughs.

'No, I'm not,' I tell him, laughing back.

'Yeah, I think you are. In fact, I'm totally sure of it,' he says.

'Are you?'

Trent finishes his drink, sucks on an ice cube and asks, 'So, who are you fucking?'

'No one. Who I fuck is not your business or Blair's, okay?'

'Yeah, right,' he snorts.

'What is this?' I ask Trent.

He doesn't say anything.

'Who are you fucking?' I ask him.

'Oh, come on, Clay, please.'

'No, who are you fucking, Trent?' I ask again.

'You don't get it, do you?'

'Get what? What is there to get?' I ask. 'If this has anything to do with Blair, you're really screwed. She should know better. Does she think we're still going-out? Is that what she told you? Well, we're not, okay? Got it?' The coke's wearing off and I'm about to get up and go to the men's room.

'Have you told her?' he finally asks.

'No,' I say, still looking at him, then out the window.

'Tacky. Really tacky,' he says slowly.

'What's tacky?' Blair asks, sitting down.

'Roberto,' Trent says, averting his eyes from mine.

I don't want to leave Trent and Blair alone, so I sit there, very still.

'Oh, I don't know. I think he's friendly.'

'No, he isn't.'

'He's just different,' Blair says.

'Why do you like him?' Trent asks, finishing another ice cube, glaring at me.

'Because,' Blair says, standing up.

'Because you don't spend that much time with him.' Trent gets up also and Blair laughs and says, 'Could be,' and she's in a better mood and I start to wonder if she did any coke in the bathroom. Probably. Then I wonder if it makes any difference.

While waiting for the car to arrive, Blair and Trent smile at each other in this way that really irritates me and then she looks up at the sky, which is cloudy, and it begins to rain lightly. We get into Blair's car and she puts in a tape that she made the other night and Bananarama starts to sing and Trent asks her where the Beach-Mix tape is and Blair tells him that she burned it because she heard it too many times. For some reason I believe this and unroll the window and we drive to After Hours.

The girl I'm sitting next to at After Hours is sixteen and tan and tells me that it's tragic that KROQ has a playlist. Blair's sitting across from me and next to Trent, who's doing his Richard Blade impersonation for two young blond girls. Rip comes over, after talking to the gay porno star who's sitting at the bar with his girlfriend, and he whispers something in Blair's ear and the two of them get up and leave. The girl, who's sitting next to me, is drunk and has her hand on my thigh and is now asking if The Whiskey burned down and I tell her yeah, sure, and Blair and Rip come back and sit down and they both seem insanely alert; Blair's head moves back and forth quickly, staring at the dancers in the club; and Rip's eyes dart from side to side, looking for the girl he came with. Blair picks up a crayon and starts to write something on the table. Rip spots the girl. Tall blond boy comes over to our table and one of the girls sitting next to Trent jumps up and says, 'Teddy! I thought you were in a coma!' and Teddy explains that no, he wasn't in a coma, but that he did get his driver's license revoked for drunk driving on Pacific Coast Highway and Blair keeps drawing on the table and Teddy sits down. I think I see Julian here, leaving, and I get up from the table and go to the bar and then outside and it's raining hard and I can hear Duran Duran from inside and a girl I don't know passes by and says, 'Hi' and I nod and then go to the restroom and lock the door and stare at myself in the mirror. People knock on the door and I lean against it, don't do any of the coke, and cry for around five minutes and then I leave and walk back into the club and it's dark and crowded and nobody can see that my face is all swollen and my eyes are red and I sit down next to the drunken blond girl and she and Blair are talking about S.A.T. scores. Then Griffin comes in with this really beautiful blond girl and he flashes me a smile and the two of them go to the bar to talk to the gay porno star and his girlfriend. And somewhere along the line, Blair leaves with Rip or maybe with Trent, or maybe Rip leaves with Trent or maybe Rip leaves with the two blond girls sitting next to Trent or maybe Blair leaves with the two blond girls, and I end up dancing with this girl and she leans over to me and whispers that maybe we should go to her place. And we cross the crowded dance floor and she goes to the restroom and I wait at a table for her. Someone's written 'Help Me' over and over in red crayon on the table in a childish scrawl and there are little curlicues on the 'e's in *me*, and phone numbers written around the twenty 'Help Me's and a lot of unreadable writing around the telephone numbers and the two red words stick out even more. The girl comes back and we walk out of After Hours, past the girl who said 'hi' to me, crying in the doorway, and the gay porno star smoking a joint in the alley; past the four Mexican guys teasing the kids who go in and out of the club, and past the security officer and the parking attendant who keeps telling the Mexican boys that they'd better leave. And one of them calls out to me, 'Hey, punk faggot,' and the girl and I get into her car and drive off into the hills and we go to her room and I take off my clothes and lie on her bed and she goes into the bathroom and I wait a couple of minutes and then she finally comes out, a towel wrapped around her, and sits on the bed and I put my hands on her shoulders, and she says stop it and, after I let go, she tells me to lean against the headboard and I do and then she takes off the towel and she's naked and she reaches into the drawer by her bed and brings out a tube of Bain De Soleil and she hands it to me and then she reaches into the drawer and brings out a pair of Wayfarer sunglasses and she tells me to put them on and I do. And she takes the tube of suntan lotion from me and squeezes some onto her fingers and then touches herself and motions for me to do the same, and I do. After a while I stop and reach over to her and she stops me and says no, and then places my hand back on myself and her hand begins again and after this goes on for a while I tell her that I'm going to come and she tells me to hold on a minute and that she's almost there and she begins to move her hand faster, spreading her legs wider, leaning back against the pillows, and I take the sunglasses off and she tells me to put them back on and I put them back on and it stings when I come and then I guess she comes too. Bowie's on the stereo and she gets up, flushed, and turns the stereo off and turns on MTV. I lie there, naked, sunglasses still on, and she hands me a box of Kleenex. I wipe myself off and then look through a *Vogue* that's lying by the side of the bed. She puts a robe on and stares at me. I can hear thunder in the distance and it begins to rain harder. She lights a cigarette and I start to dress. And then I call a cab and finally take the Wayfarers off and she tells me to be quiet walking down the stairs so I won't wake her parents. The cab takes me back to Trent's apartment, and it's pouring rain outside, and when I get into my car, there's a note on the passenger seat that says, 'Have a good time?' and I'm pretty sure it's Blair's handwriting and I drive back home.

I'm sitting in my psychiatrist's office the next day, coming off from coke, sneezing blood. My psychiatrist's wearing a red V-neck sweater with nothing on underneath and a pair of cut-off jeans. I start to cry really hard. He looks at me and fingers the gold necklace that hangs from his tan neck. I stop crying for a minute and he looks at me some more and then writes something down on his pad. He asks me something. I tell him I don't know what's wrong; that maybe it has something to do with my parents but not really or maybe my friends or that I drive sometimes and get lost; maybe it's the drugs.

'At least you realize these things. But that's not what

I'm talking about, that's not really what I'm asking you, not really.'

He gets up and walks across the room and straightens a framed cover of a *Rolling Stone* with Elvis Costello on the cover and the words 'Elvis Costello Repents' in large white letters. I wait for him to ask me the question.

'Like him? Did you see him at the Amphitheater? Yeah? He's in Europe now, I guess. At least that's what I heard on MTV. Like the last album?'

'What about me?'

'What about you?'

'What about me?'

'You'll be fine.'

'I don't know,' I say. 'I don't think so.'

'Let's talk about something else.'

'What about me?' I scream, choking.

'Come on, Clay,' the psychiatrist says. 'Don't be so . . . mundane.'

It was my grandfather's birthday and we had been in Palm Springs for close to two months; for too long. The sun was hot and the air was thick during those weeks. It was lunchtime and we were all sitting out beneath the overhang in front of the pool at the old house. I could remember that my grandmother had bought me a bag of rock candy that day and I had been chewing them constantly, nervously. The housekeeper brought out cold cuts and beer and Hawaiian Punch and potato chips on a large wooden platter, and set it down on the table my aunt and my grandmother and grandfather and mother and father and I were sitting at. My mother and aunt picked at the turkey sandwiches. My grandfather was wearing a jockstrap and a straw hat and drank Michelob beer. My aunt was fanning herself with a People magazine. My grandmother hadn't been feeling well and she nibbled at her sandwich lightly and sipped cold herb tea. My mother wasn't listening to any of the conversation. She was watching my sisters and cousins play in the pool, her eyes fixated on the cool aqua water.

'I think we've been here too long,' my aunt said.

'That is an understatement,' my father said, shifting in his chair.

'I want to leave,' my aunt said in a wry far-off voice, eyes distant, her fingers clenched around the magazine.

'Well,' my grandfather spoke up. 'We'd better get out of here before too soon. I'm turning as red as a tamale. Right, Clay?' He winked at me and opened his fifth beer.

'I'm going to make flight reservations today,' my aunt said.

One of my cousins was looking through a copy of the L.A. Times and mentioned something about a plane crash in San Diego. Everybody murmured, and plans for leaving were forgotten.

'How awful,' my aunt said.

'I think I would rather die in a plane crash than any other way,' my father said after some time.

'I think it would be dreadful.'

'But it would be nothing. You get bombed on the plane, take a Librium, and the plane takes off and crashes and you never know what hit you.' My father crossed his legs.

It was silent at the table. The only sounds came from my sisters and cousins splashing in the water.

'What do you think?' my aunt asked my mother.

'I try not to think about things like that,' my mother said.

'What about you, Mom?' my father asked my grandmother.

My grandmother, who hadn't said anything all day, wiped her mouth and said very quietly, 'I wouldn't want to die in any way.'

I drive over to Trent's house, but Trent, I remember, is in Palm Springs, so I drive to Rip's place and some blond kid answers the door only wearing a bathing suit, the sunlamp in the living room burning. 'Rip is gone,' the blond kid says. I leave, and as I'm pulling onto Wilshire, Rip pulls in front of me in his Mercedes, and leans out the window and says, 'Spin and I are going to City Cafe. Meet us there.' I nod, follow Rip down Melrose, the license plate that reads 'CLIMAXX' shimmering.

City Cafe is closed and there's an old man in ragged clothing and an old black hat on, talking to himself, standing in front and when we pull up, he scowls at us. Rip unrolls his window and I drive up alongside him.

'Where do you want to go?' I ask him.

'Spin wants to go to Hard Rock.'

'I'll follow you,' I tell him.

It starts to rain. We get to Hard Rock Cafe and once

we're seated, Spin tells me that he got some great stuff this afternoon. There's a man sitting at the table next to ours whose eyes are closed very tightly. The girl he's sitting with doesn't seem to mind and picks at a salad. When the man finally opens his eyes, I'm relieved for some reason. Spin's still talking and when I try to change the subject and ask where Julian might be, Spin tells me that he once got ripped off on what was otherwise real good blow from Julian. Rip tells me that Julian has too many hang-ups.

'For one, he is constantly strung out.'

Spin looks at me and nods. 'Strung out.'

'I mean he sells great coke and smack, but he shouldn't sell it to junior high kids. That's real low.'

'Yeah,' I say, taking this in. 'Low.'

'Some people say that that thirteen-year-old kid who O.D.'d at Beverly bought the smack from Julian.'

I turn to Rip after a while. 'What have you been doing?'

'Not too much. Took some animal tranquilizers last night with Warren and went to see The Grimsoles,' he says. 'They were cool. Throwing rats out into the audience. Warren took one out to the car.' Rip looks down, giggles. 'And killed it. Big rat too. Took him twenty, thirty minutes to kill the fucker.'

'I just got back from Vegas,' Spin says. 'Derf and I drove down. Just hung out at my father's hotel by the pool in our jocks. It was cool . . . I guess.'

'What have you been doing, dude?' Rip asks.

'Oh, not too much,' I say.

'Yeah, there's not a whole lot to do anymore,' he says.

Spin agrees, nods.

After dinner we share a joint in the car as we drive out to Malibu to buy a couple of grams of coke from some guy named Dead. I'm sitting in the small backseat of Rip's car and I thought that Rip had said, 'We're going to meet someone called Ed.' But when Spin said, 'How do you know Dead is gonna be around?' and Rip said, 'Because Dead is always around,' I realized what the name was.

It seems that there's a party at Dead's house and some of the people there, mostly young boys, look at the three of us strangely, probably because Rip and Spin and I aren't wearing bathing suits. We walk up to Dead, who's in his midforties, wearing a pair of briefs, lying in a huge pile of pillows, two tan young boys sitting by his side watching HBO, and Dead hands Rip a large envelope. There's a blond pretty girl in a bikini sitting behind Dead and she's petting the head of the boy who's on Dead's left.

'You gotta be more careful, boys,' Dead lisps.

'Why's that, Dead?' Rip asks.

'There are narcs crawling all over the Colony.'

'No. Really?' Spin asks.

'Yeah. Kid of mine was shot in the leg by a narc.'

'No way. Really?'

'Yeah.'

'Jesus.'

'The guy was seventeen, for Christ's sake. Shot in the fucking leg. Maybe you know him.'

'Who was it?' Rip asks. 'Christian?'

'No. Randall. Goes to Oakwood. Huh?'

Spin shakes his head and 'Hungry Like the Wolf' bursts out of the speakers that are attached to the ceiling, above Dead's balding, sweaty head.

'You gotta be more careful.'

'Yeah. You gotta be more careful,' Spin says, licking his lips at the girl whose fingers are still running through the blond boy's hair. Blond boy winks at me, pouts his lips.

In the car, Spin tastes the coke and says that it's cut with too much novocaine. Rip says that at this point he doesn't care and that he just wants to do some. Rip turns the radio up and keeps screaming happily 'What's gonna happen to all of us?' And Spin keeps screaming back, 'All of who, dude? All of who?' We do some of the coke and then go to an arcade in Westwood and play video games for close to two hours and end up spending something like twenty bucks apiece and we stop playing only because we run out of quarters. Rip only has one-hundred-dollar bills on him and the arcade won't give him change. So Rip stuffs the bills back into his pocket and yells fuck off to the guy working at the change booth and the three of us go back to his car and finish the rest of the coke.

Blair's father is having this party for a young Australian actor whose new film is opening in L.A. next week. Blair's dad is trying to get the actor to star in the new film he's producing, some thirty-million-dollar science-fiction adventure film called *Star Raiders*. But the Australian actor's price is too high. I go to the party to try to talk to Blair, but I haven't seen her yet, only a lot of actors and

Blair's friends from film school at U.S.C. Jared's there and he keeps trying to pick up on the Australian actor. Jared keeps asking him if he's seen 'The Twilight Zone' with Agnes Moorehead, and the Australian actor keeps shaking his head and saying, 'No, mate.' Jared mentions other episodes of the show and the Australian actor, who's sweating profusely and drinking his fourth rum and Coke, keeps telling Jared that he hasn't seen any of 'The Twilight Zone' episodes he's talking about. Finally, the actor walks away from Jared, and Jared's joined by his new boyfriend, not the waiter from Morton's but a costume designer who worked on Blair's father's last film, and who might, or might not, work on the costumes for *Star Raiders*. The Australian actor walks over to his wife, who ignores him. Kim tells me that the two of them got into a fight this afternoon and that she left their bungalow at the Beverly Hills Hotel in a rage and went to an expensive hair salon on Rodeo and had all her hair chopped off. Her hair's red and cut close to the scalp and when she turns her head to a different angle, I can catch patches of white beneath the spiked hair.

Talk of the damage the storms caused at Malibu is brought up and someone mentions that the entire house next to theirs collapse. 'Just like that. One minute it was there. The next – whoosh . . . Just like that.' Blair's mother nods her head as she listens to the director who's telling her this and her lips are trembling and she keeps glancing over at Jared. I'm about to go over and ask her where Blair is, but some people, a couple of actors and actresses and a director and some studio executives enter, and Blair's mother walks over to them. They've just come from the

Golden Globe Awards. One of the actresses sweeps into the room and hugs the costume designer and whispers to him loudly, 'Marty just lost, get him a whiskey neat, fast, and get me a vodka collins before I collapse, will you, darling?'

The costume designer snaps his fingers at the black, gray-haired bartender and says, 'Did you hear that?' The bartender rises out of his stupor a little too quickly, a little too unconvincingly and makes the actress her drinks. People begin to ask her who won what at the Golden Globes. But the actress and most of the actors and producers and studio executives have forgotten. The director, Marty, remembers and he recites each name carefully and if someone asks who they were up against, the director will look straight ahead and tell them, in alphabetical order.

I start to talk to one of the boys who goes to film school at U.S.C. He's very tan and has the beginnings of a blond beard and wears glasses and ripped Tretorn tennis shoes and he keeps talking about the 'aesthetic indifference' in American movies. The two of us are sitting alone in the den and soon Alana and Kim and Blair walk in. They sit down. Blair doesn't look at me. Kim touches the boy from film school's leg and says, 'I called you last night, where were you?' And he says, 'Jeff and I smoked a couple of bowls and then went to a screening of the new *Friday the 13th* movie.' I look over at Blair, try to make eye contact, get her attention. But she won't look over at me.

Jared and Blair's father and the director of *Star Raiders* and the costume designer walk in and sit down and the talk soon turns to the Australian actor and Blair's father asks the director, who's wearing a Polo sweatsuit and dark glasses, why the actor is in town.

'I think he's here to see if he got nominated for an Oscar. The nominations come out soon, you know.'

'For that piece of shit?' Blair's father barks.

He calms down and looks over at Blair, who sits by the fireplace, near where the Christmas tree used to be, and she looks depressed. Her father motions for her. 'Come here, baby, sit on Daddy's lap.' And Blair stares at him incredulously for a moment and then looks down, smiles and walks out of the room. No one says anything. After a while the director clears his throat and says that if they can't get that 'fuckin' Aussie' to be in *Star Raiders*, then who's going to star in it? Some names go around.

'What about that delicious boy who was in *Beastman!*? You know who I'm talking about, Clyde.' The costume designer looks over at the director, who's scratching his chin, deep in thought.

Blair walks back in with a drink and looks over at me and I look away and pretend to be interested in the conversation.

The costume designer slaps his knee and says, 'Marco! Marco!' He yelps the name again. 'Marco . . . uh, Marco . . . Ferr . . . Ferra . . . oh shit, I have completely forgotten.'

'Marco King?'

'No, no, no.'

'Marco Katz?'

Exasperated, the costume designer shakes his head and says, 'Did anyone see *Beastman!*?'

'When did *Beastman!* come out?' Blair's father asks.

'*Beastman!* came out last fall, I think.'

'Did it? I thought I saw it at the Avco over the summer.'

'But I saw a screening of it over at MGM.'

'It didn't even open at the Avco,' someone says.

'I think you're talking about Marco Ferraro,' Blair says.

'Yeah, that's it,' the costume designer says. 'Marco Ferraro.'

'I thought he O.D.'d,' Jared says.

'Yeah, *Beastman!*, that was pretty good,' the film student says to me. 'See it?'

I nod, looking over at Blair. I didn't like *Beastman!* and I ask the film student, 'Didn't it bother you the way they just kept dropping characters out of the film for no reason at all?'

The film student pauses and says, 'Kind of, but that happens in real life . . .'

I stare ahead, at Blair.

'I mean, doesn't it?'

'I guess.' She won't look at me.

'Marco Ferraro?' Blair's father asks. 'Is he a dago?'

'He's gorgeous,' Kim sighs.

'Total babe,' Alana nods.

'Really?' the director asks, grinning, leaning toward Kim. 'Who else do you think is . . . gorgeous?'

'Yeah, girls,' Blair's father says. 'Maybe you can give us some input.'

'Just remember,' Jared says. 'No great actors. Just some guy whose ass looks as good as his face.'

The costume designer nods and says, 'Absolutely.'

'Daddy, you know I've been asking you to put Adam Ant or Sting in the movie,' Blair says.

'I know, I know, honey. Clyde and I have been talking it over and if you really want it that bad, I think something can be arranged. What do you think about Adam Ant or Sting in *Star Raiders?*' he asks Alana and Kim.

'I'd see it,' Kim says.

'I'd see it twice,' Alana says.

'I'd get it on videocassette,' Kim adds.

'I agree with Blair,' Blair's father says. 'I think we should seriously look into Adam Ant or String.'

'That's Sting, Daddy.'

'Yeah, Sting.'

Clyde smiles and looks at Kim. 'Yeah, let's get Sting. Whaddya think about that, honey?'

Kim blushes and says, 'That would be great.'

'We'll call him and Adam for readings next week.'

'Thank you, Daddy,' Blair says.

'Anything you want, baby.'

'You better check his bod out first, Clyde,' says Jared, looking concerned.

'Oh, we will, we will,' Clyde says, still smiling at Kim. 'Wanna be there when we do it?'

Blair finally looks at me with this pained look in her eyes and I look over at Kim, almost ashamed, then angry.

Kim blushes once more and says, 'Maybe.'

Julian hasn't called me since I gave him the money and so I decide to call him the next day. But I don't have his number and so I call Rip, but Rip's gone, some young kid tells me so I call Trent's apartment and Chris answers and tells me that Trent's still in Palm Springs and then asks if

I know anyone who has any meth. I finally call Blair and she gives me Julian's number and when I'm about to tell her that I'm sorry about the night at After Hours, she says she's got to go and hangs up. I call the number and a girl with a really familiar voice answers.

'He's either in Malibu or Palm Springs.'

'Doing what?'

'I don't know.'

'Look, can I have the number at either of those places?'

'All I know is that he's staying at the house in Rancho Mirage or at the house in the Colony.' She stops and seems unsure. 'That's all I know.' There's a long pause. 'Who is this? Finn?'

'Finn? No. I just need the number.'

There's another pause and then a sigh. 'Okay, listen. I don't know where he is. Oh, shit . . . I can't tell you this. Who is this?'

'Clay.'

There's a longer pause.

'Listen,' I say. 'Don't tell him I called. I'll just get in touch with him later.'

'You sure?'

'Yeah.' I start to hang up.

'Finn?' she asks.

I hang up.

That night I go to a party at Kim's house and end up meeting someone, Evan, who tells me that he's a close friend of Julian's. And the next day we go to McDonald's after he gets out of school. It's around three in the afternoon, and Evan sits across from me.

'So, is Julian in Palm Springs?' I ask him.

'Palm Springs is great,' Evan says.

'Yeah,' I say. 'Do you know if he's there?'

'I love it. It's the most fuckin' beautiful place in the world. Maybe you and I can go up there sometime,' he says.

'Yeah, sometime.' What does that mean?

'Yeah. It's great. So's Aspen. Aspen's hot.'

'Is Julian there?'

'Julian?'

'Yeah, I heard he might be down there.'

'Why would Julian be at Aspen?'

I tell him I have to go to the restroom. Evan says sure. I go to the phone instead and call Trent, who got back from Palm Springs and ask him if he saw Julian there. He tells me no and that the coke he got from Sandy sucks and that he has too much of it and he can't sell it. I tell Trent that I can't find Julian and that I'm strung out and tired. He asks me where I am.

'In a McDonald's in Sherman Oaks,' I tell him.

'That's why,' Trent says.

I don't understand and hang up.

Rip says you can always find someone at Pages at one or two in the morning in Encino. Rip and I drive there one night because Du-par's is crowded with teenage boys coming from toga parties and old waitresses wearing therapeutic shoes and lilacs pinned to their uniforms who keep telling people to be quiet. So Rip and I go to Pages and Billy and Rod are there and so are Simon and Amos and LeDeu and Sophie and Kristy and David. Sophie sits with us and brings over LeDeu and David. Sophie tells us about the Vice Squad concert at The Palace and says that her brother slipped her a bad lude before the show and so she slept through it. LeDeu and David are in a band called Western Survival and they both seem calm and cautious. Rip asks Sophie where someone named Boris is and she tells him that he's at the house in Newport. LeDeu has this huge mass of black hair, really stiff and sticking out in all directions, and he tells me that whenever he goes to Du-par's, people always move away from him. That's why he and David always come to Pages. Sophie falls asleep on my shoulder and soon my arm falls asleep, but I don't move it since her head's on it. David's wearing sunglasses and a Fear T-shirt and tells me that he saw me at Kim's New Year's Eve party. I nod and tell him I remember even though he wasn't there.

We talk about new music and the state of L.A. bands and the rain and Rip makes faces at an old Mexican couple sitting across from us; he leers at them and slides the black fedora he's wearing over his face and grins. I excuse myself and go to the bathroom. Two jokes written on the bathroom wall at Pages: How do you get a nun pregnant? Fuck her. What's the difference between a J.A.P. and a bowl of spaghetti? Spaghetti moves when you eat it. And below the jokes: 'Julian gives great head. And is dead.'

Almost everybody had gone home that last week in the desert. Only my grandfather and grandmother, mother and father and myself were left. All the maids had gone, as had the gardener and the poolman. My sisters went to San Francisco with my aunt and her children. Everybody was very tired of Palm Springs. We had been there off and on for nine weeks and nowhere else except Rancho Mirage for the past three. Nothing much happened during the last week. One day, a couple of days before we left, my grandmother went into town with my mother and bought a blue purse. My parents took her to a party at a director's house that night. I stayed in the big house with my grandfather, who had gotten drunk and had fallen asleep earlier that evening. The artifcial waterfall in the spacious pool had been turned off, and with the exception of the jacuzzi, the pool itself was in the process of being drained. Someone had found a rattlesnake floating on top of what was left of the water at the bottom, and my parents warned me to stay in the house and not go out into the desert.

That night it was very warm and while my grandfather slept I ate steak and ribs that had been flown down two days earlier from one of the hotels my grandfather owned in Nevada. I watched a rerun of 'The Twilight Zone' that night and took a walk. No one was out. The palm trees were trembling and the street lights were very bright and if

*you looked past the house and into the desert, all there was
was blackness. No cars passed and I thought I saw a
rattlesnake slither into the garage. The darkness, the wind,
the rustling from the hedges, the empty cigarette box lying
on the driveway all had an eerie effect on me and I ran
inside and turned all the lights on and got into bed and fell
asleep, listening to the strange desert wind moan outside my
window.*

It's late on a Saturday night and we're all over at Kim's
house. There's nothing much to do here, except drink gin
and tonics and vodka with lots of lime juice and watch
old movies on the Betamax. I keep staring at this portrait
of Kim's mother which hangs over the bar in the high-
ceilinged living room. There's nothing much happening
tonight except that Blair has heard about the New Garage
downtown between 6th and 7th or 7th and 8th and so
Dimitri and Kim and Alana and Blair and I decide to
drive downtown.

The New Garage is actually a club that's in a four-story
parking lot; the first and second and third floors are
deserted and there are still a couple of cars parked there
from the day before. The fourth story is where the club is.
The music's loud and there are a lot of people dancing
and the entire floor smells like beer and sweat and
gasoline. The new Icicle Works single comes on and a
couple of The Go-Go's are there and so is one of The
Blasters and Kim says that she spotted John Doe and

Exene standing by the DJ. Alana starts to talk to a couple of English boys she knows who work at Fred Segal. Kim talks to me. She tells me that she doesn't think that Blair likes me much anymore. I shrug and look out an open window. From where I'm standing, I look out the window and out into the night, at the tops of buildings in the business district, dark, with an occasional lighted room somewhere near the top. There's a huge cathedral with a large, almost monolithic lighted cross standing on the roof and pointing toward the moon; a moon which seems rounder and more grotesquely yellow than I remember. I look at Kim for a moment and don't say anything. I spot Blair on the dance floor with some pretty young boy, maybe sixteen, seventeen, and they both look really happy. Kim says that it's too bad, though I don't think she means it. Dimitri, drunk and mumbling incoherently, shambles over to the two of us, and I think he's going to say something to Kim, but instead he sticks his hand through the window, getting the skin stuck on the glass, and as he tries to pull his hand away, it becomes all cut up, mutilated, and blood begins to spurt out unevenly, splashing thickly onto the glass. After taking him to some emergency room at some hospital, we go to a coffee shop on Wilshire and sit there until about four and then we go home.

There's another religious program on before I'm supposed to go out with Blair. The man who's talking has gray hair, pink-tinted sunglasses and very wide lapels on

his jacket and he's holding a microphone. A neon-lit
Christ stands forlornly in the background. 'You feel confused. You feel frustrated,' he tells me. 'You don't know
what's going on. That's why you feel hopeless, helpless.
That's why you feel there is no way out of the situation.
But Jesus will come. He will come through the eye of that
television screen. Jesus will put a roadblock in your life so
that you can turn around and He's gonna do it for you
now. Heavenly Father, You will set the captive free. They,
who are in bondage, teach them. Celebrate the Lord. Let
this be a night of Deliverance. Tell Jesus, "Forgive me of
my sins," and then you may feel the joy that is unspeak-
able. May your cup overflow. In Jesus' name, Amen . . .
Hallelujah!'

I wait for something to happen. I sit there for close to
an hour. Nothing does. I get up, do the rest of the coke
that's in my closet and stop at the Polo Lounge for a
drink before picking up Blair, who I called earlier and
mentioned that I had two tickets to a concert at the
Amphitheater and she didn't say anything except 'I'll go'
and I told her I'd pick her up at seven and she hung up. I
tell myself, while I sit alone at the bar that I was going to
call one of the numbers that flashed on the bottom of the
screen. But I realized that I didn't know what to say. And
I remember seven of the words that the man spoke. Let
this be a night of Deliverance.

I remember these words for some reason as Blair and I
are sitting at Spago after having just seen the concert and
it's late and we're sitting by ourselves on the patio and
Blair sighs and asks for a cigarette. We drink Champagne
Kirs, but Blair has too many and when she orders her

sixth, I tell her that maybe she's had enough and she looks at me and says, 'I am hot and thirsty and I will order what I fucking want.'

I'm sitting with Blair in an Italian ice-cream parlor in Westwood. Blair and I eat some Italian ice cream and talk. Blair mentions that *Invasion of the Body Snatchers* is on cable this week.

'The original?' I ask, wondering why she's talking about that movie. I start making paranoid connections.

'No.'

'The remake?' I ask cautiously.

'Yeah.'

'Oh.' I look back at my ice cream, which I'm not eating much of.

'Did you feel the earthquake?' she asks.

'What?'

'Did you feel the earthquake this morning?'

'An earthquake?'

'Yes.'

'This morning?'

'Yeah.'

'No, I didn't.'

Pause. 'I thought maybe you had.'

In the parking lot I turn to her and say, 'Listen, I'm sorry, really,' even though I'm not too sure if I am.

'Don't,' she says. 'It's okay.'

At a red light on Sunset, I lean over and kiss her and she puts the car into second and speeds up. On the radio is a song I have already heard five times today but hum along to anyway. Blair lights a cigarette. We pass a poor woman with dirty, wild hair and a Bullock's bag sitting by her side full of yellowed newspapers. She's squatting on a sidewalk by the freeway, her face tilted toward the sky; eyes half-slits, because of the glare of the sun. Blair locks the doors and then we're driving along a side street up in the hills. No cars pass by. Blair turns the radio up. She doesn't see the coyote. It's big and brownish gray and the car hits it hard as it runs out into the middle of the street and Blair screams and tries to drive on, the cigarette falling from her lips. But the coyote is stuck under the wheels and it's squealing and the car is having difficulty moving. Blair stops the car and puts it in reverse and turns the engine off. I don't want to get out of the car, but Blair's crying hysterically, her head in her lap, and I get out of the car and walk slowly over to the coyote. It's lying on its side, trying to wag its tail. Its eyes are wide and frightened looking and I watch it start to die beneath the sun, blood running out of its mouth. All of its legs are smashed and its body keeps convulsing and I begin to notice the pool of blood that's forming at the head. Blair calls out to me, and I ignore her and watch the coyote. I stand there for ten minutes. No cars pass. The coyote shudders and arches its body up three, four times and then its eyes go white. Flies start to converge, skimming over the blood and the drying film of the eyes. I walk back to the car and Blair drives off and when we get to her house she turns on the TV and I think she takes some Valium or some Thorazine and the two of us go to bed while 'Another World' starts.

And at Kim's party that night, while everyone plays Quarters and gets drunk, Blair and I sit on a couch in the living room and listen to an old XTC album and Blair tells me that maybe we should go out to the guest house and we get up and leave the living room and walk by the lighted pool and once inside the guest house we kiss roughly and I've never wanted her more and she grabs my back and pushes me against her so hard that I lose my balance and we both fall, slowly, to our knees and her hands push up beneath my shirt and I can feel her hand, smooth and cool on my chest and I kiss, lick, her neck and then her hair, which smells like jasmine, and I rub against her and we push each other's jeans down and touch each other and I rub my hand through her underwear and when I enter her too quickly, she breathes in sharply and I try to be very still.

I'm sitting in Trumps with my father. He's bought a new Ferrari and has started wearing a cowboy hat. He doesn't wear the cowboy hat into Trumps, which relieves me, sort of. He wants me to see his astrologer and advises me to buy the Leo Astroscope for the upcoming year.

'I will.'

'Those planetary vibes work on your body in weird ways,' he's saying.

'I know.'

The window we're sitting next to is open and I lift a glass of champagne to my mouth and close my eyes and let my hair get slightly ruffled by the hot winds and then I turn my head and look up toward the hills. A businessman stops by. I had asked my mother to come, but she said that she was busy. She was lying out by the pool reading *Glamour* magazine when I asked her to come.

'Just for drinks,' I said.

'I don't want to go to Trumps "just for drinks."'

I sighed, said nothing.

'I don't want to go anywhere.'

One of my sisters, who was lying next to her, shrugged and put on her sunglasses.

'Anyway, I'm having ON put on the cable,' she said, harassed, as I left the pool.

The businessman leaves. My father doesn't say much. I try to make conversation. I tell him about the coyote that Blair ran over. He tells me that it's too bad. He keeps looking out the window, eyeing the fire-hydrant-red Ferrari. My father asks me if I'm looking forward to going back to New Hampshire and I look at him and tell him yes.

I awoke to the sound of voices outside. The director whose party my parents had taken my grandmother to the night before was outside at the table, under the umbrella, eating brunch. The director's wife was sitting by his side. My grandmother looked well under the shade of the umbrella. The director began to talk about the death of a stuntman on one of his films. He talked about how he missed a step. Of how he fell headfirst onto the pavement below.

'He was a wonderful boy. He was only eighteen.'

My father opened another beer.

My grandfather looked down, sadly. 'What was his name?' he asked.

'What?' The director glanced up.

'What was his name? What was the kid's name?'

There was a long silence and I could only feel the desert breeze and the sound of the jacuzzi beating and the pool draining and Frank Sinatra singing 'Summer Wind' and I prayed that the director remembered the name. For some reason it seemed very important to me. I wanted very badly for the director to say the name. The director opened his mouth and said, 'I forgot.'

From lunch with my father I drive to Daniel's house. The maid answers the door and leads me out to the backyard, where Daniel's mother, who I met at Parents Day at Camden in New Hampshire, is playing tennis in her bikini, her body greased with tanning oil. She stops playing tennis with the ball machine and she walks over to me and talks about Japan and Aspen and then about a strange dream she had the other night where Daniel was kidnapped. She sits down on a chaise longue by the pool and the maid brings her an iced tea and Daniel's mother takes the lemon out of it and sucks on it while staring at a young blond boy raking leaves out of the pool and then she tells me she has a migraine and that she hasn't seen Daniel in days. I walk inside and up the stairs and past the poster of Daniel's father's new film and into Daniel's room to wait for him. When it becomes apparent that Daniel won't be coming home, I get into my car and drive over to Kim's house to pick up my vest.

The first thing I hear when I enter the house is screaming. The maid doesn't seem to mind and she walks back into the kitchen after opening the door for me. The house is still not furnished yet and as I walk out to the pool, I pass the Nazi pots. It's Muriel who's screaming. I walk out to where she's lying with Kim and Dimitri by the pool and she stops. Dimitri's wearing black Speedos and a sombrero and is holding an electric guitar, trying to play 'L.A. Woman,' but he can't play the guitar too well because his hand was recently rebandaged after he sliced it open at the New Garage and every time his hand comes down on the guitar, his face flinches. Muriel screams again. Kim's smoking a joint and she finally notices me and gets up and tells me that she thought her mother was in England but she recently read in *Variety* that she's actually in Hawaii scouting locations with the director of her next film.

'You should call before you come over,' Kim tells me, handing Dimitri the joint.

'I've tried, but no one answers,' I lie, realizing that probably no one would have answered the phone even if I had called.

Muriel screams and Kim looks over at her, distracted and says, 'Well, maybe you've been calling the numbers that I've disconnected.'

'Maybe,' I tell her. 'I'm sorry. I just came for my vest.'

'Well, I just . . . it's okay this once, but I don't like people coming over. Someone is telling people where I live. I don't like it.'

'I'm sorry about that.'

'I mean, I used to like people coming over, but now I just can't stand it. I can't take it.'

'When are you going back to school?' I ask her as we walk back to her room.

'I don't know.' She gets defensive. 'Has it even started yet?'

We walk into her room. There's only a big mattress on the floor and a huge, expensive stereo that takes up an entire wall and a poster of Peter Gabriel and a pile of clothes in the corner. There are also the pictures that were taken at her New Year's Eve party tacked up over the mattress. I see one of Muriel shooting up, wearing my vest, me watching. Another of me standing in the living room only wearing a T-shirt and my jeans, trying to open a bottle of champagne, looking totally out of it. Another of Blair lighting a cigarette. One of Spit, wasted, beneath the flag. From outside, Muriel screams and Dimitri keeps trying to play the guitar.

'What have you been doing?' I ask.

'What have you been doing?' she asks back.

I don't say anything.

She looks up, bewildered. 'Come on, Clay, tell me.' She looks through the pile of clothes. 'You must do something.'

'Oh, I don't know.'

'What do you do?' she asks.

'Things, I guess.' I sit on the mattress.

'Like what?'

'I don't know. Things.' My voice breaks and for a moment I think about the coyote and I think that I'm going to cry, but it passes and I just want to get my vest and get out of here.

'For instance?'

'What's your mom doing?'

'Narrating a documentary about teenage spastics. What do you do, Clay?'

Someone's written the alphabet, maybe Spit or Jeff or Dimitri, on her wall. I try to concentrate on that, but I notice that most of the letters aren't in order and so I ask, 'What else is your mom doing?'

'She's going to do this movie in Hawaii. What do you do?'

'Have you spoken to her?'

'Don't ask me about my mother.'

'Why not?'

'Don't say that.'

'Why not?' I say again.

She finds the vest. 'Here.'

'Why not?'

'What do you do?' she asks, holding out the vest.

'What do you do?'

'What do you do?' she asks, her voice shaking. 'Don't ask me, please. Okay, Clay?'

'Why not?'

She sits on the mattress after I get up. Muriel screams. 'Because . . . I don't know,' she sighs.

I look at her and don't feel anything and walk out with my vest.

Rip and I are sitting in I.R.S. Records on La Brea. Some executive in charge of promotion is scoring some coke from Rip. The guy who's executive in charge of promotion is twenty-two and has platinum-blond hair and is wearing all white. Rip wants to know what he can get him.

'Need some coke,' the guy says.

'Great,' Rip says, and reaches into the pocket of his Parachute jacket.

'It's a nice day out,' the guy says.

'Yeah, it's great,' Rip says.

'Great,' I say.

Rip asks the guy if he can get him a backstage pass to The Fleshtones concert.

'Sure.' He hands Rip two small envelopes.

Rip says that he'll talk to him later, sometime soon, and hands him an envelope.

'Great,' the guy says.

Rip and I get up and Rip asks him, 'Have you seen Julian?'

The guy is sitting behind a large desk and he picks up the phone and tells Rip to wait a minute. The guy doesn't say anything into the phone. Rip leans on the desk and picks up a demo of some new British group that's on the large glass desk. The guy gets off the phone and Rip hands the demo to me. I study it and put it back on the desk. The guy grins and tells Rip that the two of them should have lunch.

'What about Julian?' Rip asks.

'I don't know,' the executive in charge of promotion says.

'Thanks a lot.' Rip winks.

'Great, you bet, babe,' the guy says, leaning back in the chair, his eyes slowly turning up.

Trent calls me up while Blair and Daniel are over at my house and invites us to a party in Malibu; he mentions something about X dropping by. Blair and Daniel say that it sounds like a good idea and though I really don't want to go to a party or see Trent all that badly, the day is clear and a ride to Malibu seems like a nice idea. Daniel wants to go anyway to see what houses were destroyed in the rainstorms. Driving down Pacific Coast Highway, I'm really careful not to speed and Blair and Daniel talk about the new U2 album and when the new song by The Go-Go's comes on they ask me to turn it up and sing along with it, half joking, half serious. It gets cooler as we drive nearer the ocean and the sky turns purplish, gray, and we pass an ambulance and two police cars parked by the side of the road as we head toward the darkness of Malibu and Daniel cranes his neck to get a look and I slow down a little. Blair says she suspects that they're searching for a wreck, an accident, and the three of us are silent for a moment.

X is not at the party in Malibu. Neither are too many other people. Trent answers the door wearing a pair of briefs and he tells us that he and a friend are using this guy's place while he's in Aspen. Apparently, Trent comes here a lot and so do a lot of his friends, who are mostly blond-haired pretty male models like Trent, and he starts to tell us to help ourselves to a drink and some food and he walks back to the jacuzzi and lies down, stretches out under the darkening sky. There are mostly young boys in the house and they seem to be in every room and they all look the same: thin, tan bodies, short blond hair, blank look in the blue eyes, same empty toneless voices, and then I start to wonder if I look exactly like them. I try to forget about it and get a drink and look around the living room. Two boys are playing Ms. Pac Man. Another boy lying in an overstuffed couch smoking a joint and watching MTV. One of the boys playing Ms. Pac Man moans and hits the machine, hard.

There are two dogs running along the empty beach. One of the blond boys call out to them, 'Hanoi, Saigon, come here,' and the dogs, both Dobermans, come leaping gracefully onto the deck. The boy pets them and Trent smiles and starts to complain about the service at Spago. The boy who hit the Ms. Pac Man machine walks over and looks down at Trent.

'I need the keys to the Ferrari. I'm going to get some booze. Know where the credit cards are?'

'Just charge it,' Trent says wearily. 'And get lots of tonic, okay, Chuck?'

'Keys?'

'Car.'

'Sure thing.'

The sun starts to break through the clouds and the boy with the dogs sits next to Trent and begins to talk to us. It seems that the boy is also a model and is trying to break into the movie business, like Trent. But the only thing his agent's gotten him is a Carl's Jr. commercial.

'Hey, Trent, it's on, dude,' a boy calls from inside the house. Trent taps me on the shoulder and winks and tells me that I have to see something; he motions for Blair and Daniel to come also. We walk into the house and down a hall and into what I guess is the master bedroom and there are about ten boys in the room, along with the four of us and the two dogs, who followed us into the house. Everyone in the room is looking up at a large television screen. I look up to the screen.

There's a young girl, nude, maybe fifteen, on a bed, her arms tied together above her head and her legs spread apart, each foot tied to a bedpost. She's lying on what looks like newspaper. The film's in black and white and scratchy and it's kind of hard to tell what she's lying on, but it looks like newspaper. The camera cuts quickly to a young, thin, nude, scared-looking boy, sixteen, maybe seventeen, being pushed into the room by this fat black guy, who's also naked and who's got this huge hard-on. The boy stares at the camera for an uncomfortably long time, this panicked expression on his face. The black man ties the boy up on the floor, and I wonder why there's a chainsaw in the corner of the room, in the background, and then has sex with him and then he has sex with the girl and then walks off the screen. When he comes back he's carrying a box. It looks like a toolbox and I'm confused for a minute and Blair walks out of the room. And he takes out an ice pick and what looks like a wire hanger and a package of nails and then a thin, large knife and he comes toward the girl and Daniel smiles and nudges me in the ribs. I leave quickly as the black man tries to push a nail into the girl's neck.

I sit in the sun and light a cigarette and try to calm down. But someone's turned the volume up and so I sit on the deck and I can hear the waves and the seagulls crying out and I can hear the hum of the telephone wires and I can feel the sun shining down on me and I listen to the sound of the trees shuffling in the warm wind and the screams of a young girl coming from the television in the master bedroom. Trent walks back outside, twenty, thirty minutes later, after the screams and yelling of the girl and the boy stop, and I notice that he has a hard-on. He adjusts himself and sits next to me.

'Guy paid fifteen thousand for it.'

The two boys who were playing Ms. Pac Man walk out onto the deck, holding drinks, and one tells Trent that he doesn't think it's real, even though the chainsaw scene was intense.

'I bet it's real,' Trent says, somewhat defensively.

I sit back in the chair and watch Blair walk along the shore.

'Yeah, I think it's real too,' the other boy says, easing himself into the jacuzzi. 'It's gotta be.'

'Yeah?' Trent asks, a little hopefully.

'I mean, like, how can you fake a castration? They cut the balls off that guy real slowly. You can't fake that,' the boy says.

Trent nods his head and thinks about it for a while and Daniel comes out, smiling, red-faced, and I sit back in the sun.

West, one of my grandfather's personal secretaries, came down that afternoon. He was hunched over, wearing a string tie and a jacket with one of my grandfather's hotels' insignia on the back of it, passing out Beechnut licorice gum. He talked about the heat and the plane ride on the Lear. He came with Wilson, another of my grandfather's aides, and he was wearing a red baseball cap, and he carried around clippings of how the weather in Nevada had been for the past two months. The men sat around and talked about baseball and drank beer and my grandmother sat there, her blouse hanging limply from her frail body, blue-and-yellow kerchief tied tightly around her neck.

Trent and I are standing around Westwood and he's telling me about how the guy came back from Aspen and kicked everyone out of the house in Malibu, so Trent's going to live with someone in the Valley for a couple of days, then he's going to go up to New York to do some shooting. And when I ask him what kind of shooting, he just shrugs and says, 'Shooting, dude, shooting.' He says that he really wants to go back to Malibu, that he misses the beach. He then asks me if I want to do some coke. I tell him that I do but not right now. Trent takes hold of my arm roughly and says, 'Why not?'

'Come on, Trent,' I tell him. 'My nose hurts.'

'It's all right. This'll make it feel better. We can go upstairs at Hamburger Hamlet.'

I look at Trent.

Trent looks at me.

It only takes five minutes and when we come back down onto the street, I don't feel too much better. Trent says that he does and wants to go to the arcade across the street. He also tells me that Sylvan, from France, O.D.'d on Friday. I tell him that I don't know who Sylvan was. He shrugs. 'Ever mainline?' he asks.

'Have I ever mainlined?'

'Yeah.'

'No.'

'Oh boy,' he says ominously.

When we get to his car, some friend's Ferrari, my nose is bleeding.

'I'll have to get you some Decadron or Celestone. They help swelling in blocked nasal passages,' he says.

'Where do you get that?' I ask, my fingers and a piece of Kleenex, covered with snot, blood. 'Where do you get that shit?'

There's a long pause and he starts the car up and says, 'Are you serious?'

My grandmother had gotten very ill that afternoon. She started to cough up blood. She had already begun to grow bald and had been losing weight as a result of pancreatic cancer. Later that night, as my grandmother lay in her bed, the others continued their conversations, talking about Mexico and bullfights and bad movies. My grandfather cut his finger opening a beer. They ordered food from an Italian restaurant in town and a boy with a patch on his jeans that read 'Aerosmith Live' delivered the food. My grandmother came down. She was feeling a little better. She didn't eat anything, though. I sat by her and my grandfather did a magic trick with two silver dollars.

'Did you see that, Grandma?' I asked. Too shy to look into her faded eyes.

'Yes. I saw it,' she said, and tried to smile.

I'm about to fall asleep, but Alana comes by unannounced and the maid lets her in and she knocks on my door and I wait a long time before I open it. She has been crying and she comes in and sits on my bed and mentions something about an abortion and starts to laugh. I don't know what to say, how to deal with it, so I tell her I'm sorry. She gets up and walks over to the window.

'Sorry?' she asks. 'What for?' She lights a cigarette but can't smoke it and puts it out.

'I don't know.'

'Well, Clay . . .' She laughs and looks out the window and I think for a minute that she's going to start to cry. I'm standing by the door and I look over at the Elvis Costello poster, at his eyes, watching her, watching us, and I try to get her away from it, so I tell her to come over here, sit down, and she thinks I want to hug her or something and she comes over to me and puts her arms around my back and says something like 'I think we've all lost some sort of feeling.'

'Was it Julian's?' I ask, tensing up.

'Julian's? No. It wasn't,' she says. 'You don't know him.'

She falls asleep and I walk downstairs, outside, and sit by the jacuzzi, looking into the lighted water, the steam coming up from it, warming me.

I get up from the pool just before dawn and walk back up to my room. Alana's standing by the window smoking a cigarette and looking out over the Valley. She tells me that she bled a lot last night and that she feels weak. We go out to breakfast in Encino and she keeps her sunglasses on and drinks a lot of orange juice. When we get back to my house, she gets out of the car and says, 'Thank you.'

'What for?' I ask.

'I don't know,' she says after a while.

She gets into her car and drives off.

When I flush the toilet in my bathroom, it becomes

stopped up with Kleenex, and blood clouds the water and I put down the lid, because there's nothing else for me to do.

I stop by Daniel's house later that day. He's sitting in his room playing Atari on his television set. He doesn't look too good, tan to the point of sunburn, younger than I remember him in New Hampshire, and when I say something to him, he'll repeat part of it and then nod. I ask him if he got the letter from Camden asking what courses he'll be taking next term and he pulls out the Pitfall cassette and puts in one called Megamania. He keeps rubbing his mouth and when I realize that he's not going to answer me, I ask him what he's been doing.

'Been doing?'

'Yeah.'

'Hanging out.'

'Hanging out where?'

'Where? Around. Pass me that joint over there on the nightstand.'

I hand him the joint and then a book of matches from The Ginger Man. He lights it and then resumes playing Megamania. He hands me the joint and I relight it. Yellow things are falling toward Daniel's man. Daniel starts to tell me about a girl he knows. He doesn't tell me her name.

'She's pretty and sixteen and she lives around here and on some days she goes to the Westward Ho on Westwood

Boulevard and she meets her dealer there. This seventeen-year-old guy from Uni. And this guy spends all day shooting her full of smack again and again . . .'

Daniel misses ducking one of the falling yellow things and it hits his man, which dissolves from the screen. He sighs, goes on. 'And then he feeds her some acid and takes her off to a party in the hills or in the Colony and then . . . and then . . .' Daniel stops.

'And then what?' I ask, handing him back the joint.

'And then she gets gangbanged by the entire party.'

'Oh.'

'What do you think?'

'That's . . . too bad.'

'Good idea for a screenplay?'

Pause. 'Screenplay.'

'Yeah. Screenplay.'

'I'm not too sure.'

He stops playing Megamania and puts in a new cassette, Donkey Kong. 'I don't think I'm going back to school,' he says. 'To New Hampshire.'

After a while I ask him why.

'I don't know.' He stops, lights the joint again. 'It doesn't seem like I've ever been there.' He shrugs, sucks in on the joint. 'It seems like I've been here for ever.' He hands it to me. I shake my head, no.

'So you're not going back?'

'I'm going to write this screenplay, see?'

'But what do your parents think?'

'My parents? They don't care. Do yours?'

'They must think something.'

'They've gone to Barbados for the month and then

they're going to oh . . . shit . . . I don't know . . . Versailles? I don't know. They don't care,' he says again.

I tell him, 'I think you should come back.'

'I really don't see the point,' Daniel says, not taking his eyes off the screen and I begin to wonder what the point was, if we ever knew. Daniel gets up finally and turns the television off and then looks out the window. 'Weird wind today. It's pretty strong.'

'What about Vanden?' I ask.

'Who?'

'Vanden. Come on Daniel. Vanden.'

'She might not be coming back,' he says, sitting back down.

'But she might.'

'Who's Vanden?'

I walk over to the window and tell him that I'm leaving in five days. There are magazines lying out by the pool and the wind moves them, sends them flying across the concrete near the pool. A magazine falls in. Daniel doesn't say anything. Before I leave I look at him lighting another joint, at the scar on his thumb and finger and feel better for some reason.

I'm in a phone booth in Beverly Hills.

'Hello?' my psychiatrist answers.

'Hi. This is Clay.'

'Yes, oh hi, Clay. Where are you?'

'In a phone booth in Beverly Hills.'

'Are you coming in today?'

'No.'

Pause.

'I see. Um, why not?'

'I don't think that you're helping me all that much.'

Another pause. 'Is that really why?'

'What?'

'Listen, why don't you —'

'Forget it.'

'Where are you in Beverly Hills?'

'I won't be seeing you anymore, I think.'

'I think I'm going to call your mother.'

'Go ahead. I really don't care. But I'm not coming back, okay?'

'Well, Clay. I don't know what to say and I know it's been difficult. Hey, man, we all have —'

'Go fuck yourself.'

On the morning of the last day, West woke up early. He was dressed in the same jacket and the same string tie, and Wilson was wearing the same red baseball cap. West offered me another piece of Bazooka bubble gum and told me that a piece of gum will make you hum and I took two pieces. He asked me if everybody was ready and I said I didn't know. The director's wife stopped by to tell us that they were flying to Las Vegas for the weekend. My grandmother was taking Percodan. We started out for the airport in the

Cadillac. In early afternoon the moment finally came to board the plane and leave the desert. Nothing was said in the empty airport lounge until my grandfather turned and looked at my grandmother and said, 'Okay, partner, let's go.' My grandmother died two months later in a large high bed in an empty hospital room on the outskirts of the desert.

Since that summer, I have remembered my grandmother in a number of ways. I remember playing cards with her and sitting on her lap in airplanes, and the way she slowly turned away from my grandfather at one of my grandfather's parties at one of his hotels when he tried to kiss her. And I remember her staying at the Bel Air Hotel and giving me pink and green mints, and at La Scala, late at night, sipping red wine, and humming 'On the Sunny Side of the Street' to herself.

I find myself standing at the gates of my elementary school. I don't remember the grass and flowers, bougain-villea I think, being there when I attended; and the asphalt that was near the administration building has been replaced by trees and the dead trees that used to hang limply over the fence near the security booth are not dead anymore; the entire parking lot has been repaved smoothly with new, black asphalt. I also don't remember a big yellow sign that reads: 'Warning. Keep Out. Guard Dogs On Duty' which hangs from the entrance gate, which is visible from my car, parked in the street outside the school. Since classes are over for the day, I decide to walk through the school.

I walk to the gate and then stop for a moment before entering, almost turning back. But I don't. I step past the gate, thinking that this is the first afternoon in a long time that I've come back and walked through the school. I watch three children climb across a jungle gym placed near the entrance gates and I spot two teachers I had in first or second grade, but I don't say anything to them. Instead, I look through the window of a classroom, where a little girl is painting a picture of the city. From where I stand, I can hear the Glee Club practicing in the room next to where the little girl paints, singing songs I forgot existed, like 'Itsy Bitsy Spider' and 'Little White Duck.'

I used to pass the school often. Every time I drove my sisters to their school, I would always make sure to drive past and I would catch sight of small children getting onto yellow buses with black trim and teachers laughing to each other in the parking lot before classes. I don't think that anyone else who went to the school drives by or gets out and looks around, since I've never seen anyone I remember. One day I saw a boy I had gone to the school with, maybe first grade, standing by the fence, alone, fingers gripping the steel wire and staring off into the distance and I told myself that the guy must live close by or something and that was why he was standing alone, like me.

I light a cigarette and sit down on a bench and notice two pay phones and remember when there used to be no pay phones. Some mothers pick their children up from school and the children catch sight of them and run across the yard and into their arms and the sight of the children running across the asphalt makes me feel peaceful; it makes me not want to get up off the bench. But I find myself walking into an old bungalow and I'm positive that this was where my third-grade classroom was located. The bungalow is in the process of being torn down. Next to the abandoned bungalow lies the old cafeteria, and it's empty and also in the process of being torn down. The paint on both buildings is faded everywhere and peeling off in huge patches of pale green.

I go to another bungalow and the door's open and I walk in. The day's homework is written on the blackboard and I read it carefully and then walk to the lockers but can't find mine. I can't remember which one it was. I go into the boy's bathroom and squeeze a soap dispenser. I pick up a yellowed magazine in the auditorium and strike a few notes on a piano. I had played the piano, the same piano, at a Christmas recital in second grade and I strike a few more chords from the song I played and they ring out through the empty auditorium and echo. I panic for some reason and leave the room. Two boys are playing handball outside. A game I forgot existed. I walk away from the school without looking back and get into my car and drive away.

I meet Julian that same day in an old rundown arcade on Westwood Boulevard. He's playing Space Invaders and I come up and stand next to him. Julian looks tired and talks slowly and I ask him where he's been and he says around and I ask him for the money and tell him that I'm leaving soon. Julian says that there are some problems, but if I come with him to this guy's place, he can give me the money.

'Who is this guy?' I ask him.

'This guy is . . .' Julian waits and blows away an entire row of Space Invaders. 'This guy is some guy I know. He'll give you your money.' Julian loses a warrior, mutters something.

'Why don't you get it from him? And then bring it to me?' I tell him.

Julian looks up from the game and stares at me.

'Wait a minute,' he says, and leaves the arcade. When he comes back, he tells me that if I want the money, I have to come with him, now.

'I really don't want to.'

'See ya later, Clay,' Julian says.

'Wait . . .'

'What's wrong? You wanna come or not? You want your money or not?'

'Why do we have to do it this way?'

'Because,' is all Julian says.

'Is there any other way we can work this out?'

Pause.

'Julian?'

'Do you want your money or not?'

'Julian.'

'Do you want your money or not, Clay?'

'Yeah.'

'Then come on, let's go.'
We leave the arcade.

Finn's apartment is on Wilshire Boulevard, not too far away from Rip's penthouse. Julian says he's known Finn for six, maybe seven months, but from the look on Julian's face I get the feeling that he's been going to Finn's apartment a lot longer than that, for too long. The parking attendant knows his car and lets him park it in the Loading Zone Only section. Julian waves at the doorman sitting on a couch. To get to Finn's place, we take the elevator and Julian presses P for Penthouse. The elevator's empty and Julian starts to sing some old Beach Boys song, really loudly, and I lean against the wall of the elevator and take a deep breath as it comes to a stop. I can make out my reflection, blond hair cut too short, a deep tan, sunglasses still on.

We walk through the darkness of the hall to get to Finn's door and Julian rings the bell. The door's opened by a boy, maybe fifteen, with bleached-blond hair and the tan, tough looks of most of the surfers at Venice or Malibu. The boy who's only wearing grey shorts, and who I recognize as the boy who was leaving Rip's apartment the day Rip was supposed to meet me at Cafe Casino, stares at us malevolently as we walk in. I wonder if this is Finn or if Finn is sleeping with this surfer and the thought makes me tense and my stomach falls a little. Julian knows where Finn's 'office' is, where Finn does his business. I start to get suspicious for some reason and nervous. Julian comes to a white door and opens it and the two of us walk into a totally spare, totally white room, complete with floor-to-ceiling windows and mirrors on the ceiling and this feeling of vertigo washes over me and I almost have to catch my balance. I notice that I can see my father's penthouse in Century City from this room and I get paranoid and start to wonder if my father can see me.

'Hey, hey, hey. It's my best boy.' Finn's sitting behind a large desk and is maybe twenty-five, thirty, blond, tan, unremarkable looking. The desk is empty except for a phone and an envelope with Finn's name on it and two small silver vials. The only other thing sitting on the desk is this glass paperweight with a small fish trapped in it, its eyes staring out helplessly, almost as if it was begging to be freed, and I start to wonder, If the fish is already dead, does it even matter?

'Who's this?' Finn asks, smiling at me.

'He's a friend of mine. Name is Clay. Clay, this is Finn.' Julian shrugs, distracted.

Finn checks me out and smiles again and then turns to Julian.

'How did everything go last night?' Finn asks, still smiling.

Julian pauses and then says, 'Okay, fine,' and looks down.

'Fine? That's all? Jason called me today and said that you were fantastic. Really tops.'

'He did?'

'Yeah. Really. He really digs you.'

I begin to feel weak, walk around the room, search my pocket for a cigarette.

Another pause and then Julian coughs.

'Well, kid, if you're not too busy today, you've got an appointment at four at the Saint Marquis with some business guy from outta town. And then tonight at Eddie's party, okay?'

Finn stares at Julian and then looks at me.

'You know what?' He starts tapping his fingers on the desk. 'You bringing your friend here might be a good thing. Guy at the Saint Marquis wants two guys. One just to watch, of course, but Jan is out at the Colony and might not be back . . .'

I look at Finn and then over at Julian.

'No, Finn. He's a friend,' Julian says. 'I owe him money. That's why I brought him by.'

'Listen, I can wait,' I say, realizing somehow that it's too late and adrenaline starts to rush through me.

'Why don't you two guys go?' Finn says, looking me over. 'Julian, take your friend.'

'No, Finn. Don't drag anybody else into this.'

'Listen, Julian,' Finn says, not smiling anymore, enunciating each word clearly. 'I said, I think that you and your friend should go to the Saint Marquis at four, all right?' Finn turns to me. 'You want your money, right?'

I shake my head, no.

'You don't?' he asks incredulously.

'Yes. I mean, yes, I . . . I do,' I say. 'Sure.'

Finn turns to Julian and then back at me. 'You feel all right?'

'Yeah,' I tell him. 'Just have the shakes.'

'Wanna lude?'

'No thanks.' I look back at the fish.

Finn turns to Julian. 'So, how are your parents, Julian?'

'I don't know.' Julian's still looking down.

'Yeah, okay . . . well,' Finn begins. 'Okay, why don't you two go to the hotel and then meet me at The Land's End and then we'll go to Eddie's party and give you your money and your friend his money. Okay, babes? How about that? How does that sound?'

'Where do I meet you?' Julian asks.

'At The Land's End. Upstairs,' Finn says. 'What is this? Is something wrong?'

'No,' Julian says. 'When?'

'Nine-thirty?'

'Fine.'

I look over at Julian and the image of Sports Club after school in fifth grade comes back to me.

'Are you okay, Julie?' Finn looks back at Julian.

'Yeah, I'm just nervous.' Julian's voice trails off. He's about to say something, mouth opens. I can hear a plane passing by, overhead. Then an ambulance.

'What is it, babe? Hey, you can tell me.' Finn seems understanding and walks over to Julian and puts his arm around him.

I think Julian's crying.

'Will you excuse us, please?' Finn asks me politely.

I walk out of the room and close the door behind me, but I can still hear the voices.

'I think that tonight will be my last . . . my last night. Okay, Finn? I don't think I can do this anymore. I'm just so sick of feeling so . . . sad all the time and I can't . . . Can't I do something else for you? Just till I pay you back?' Julian's voice is all shaky and then it cracks.

'Hey, hey, hey, baby,' Finn croons. 'Baby, it's okay.'

I could leave the penthouse now. Even though Julian drove, I could leave the penthouse. I could call someone to pick me up.

'No, Finn, no, it's not.'

'Here . . .'

'No, Finn. No way. I don't want that. I'm through with that.'

'Of course, you are.'

There's a really long silence and I can only hear a couple of matches being lit and this slapping sound, and after a while, Finn finally speaks up. 'Now, you know that you're my best boy and you know that I care for you. Just like my own kid. Just like my own son . . .' There's a pause and then Finn says, 'You look thin.'

The surfer brushes past me and enters the room and tells Finn that someone named Manuel is on the phone. The surfer leaves. Julian gets up from Finn's desk, buttoning his sleeve, and says goodbye to Finn.

'Hey, keep up the Nautilus. Keep up the bod.' Finn winks.

'Sure.'

'See ya later tonight, right, Clay?'

I want to say no, but I have the feeling somehow that I will be seeing him later tonight and I nod and say, 'Yeah' and try to sound convincing, like I mean it.

'You're terrific, you kids. Just fab,' Finn tells us.

I follow Julian across the hallway and as I cross the

living room to get to the door, I see the surfer lying in the living room on the floor, his right hand down his pants, eating a bowl of Captain Crunch. He's alternating between reading the back of the cereal box and watching 'The Twilight Zone' on the huge TV screen in the middle of the living room and Rod Serling's staring at us and tells us that we have just entered The Twilight Zone and though I don't want to believe it, it's just so surreal that I know it's true and I stare at the boy on the living-room rug for one last time and then slowly turn away and follow Julian out the door and into the darkness of Finn's hall. And in the elevator on the way down to Julian's car, I say, 'Why didn't you tell me the money was for this?' and Julian, his eyes all glassy, sad grin on his face, says, 'Who cares? Do you? Do you really care?' and I don't say anything and realize that I really don't care and suddenly feel foolish, stupid. I also realize that I'll go with Julian to the Saint Marquis. That I want to see if things like this can actually happen. And as the elevator descends, passing the second floor, and the first floor, going even farther down, I realize that the money doesn't matter. That all that does is that I want to see the worst.

The Saint Marquis. Four o'clock. Sunset Boulevard. The sun is huge and burning, an orange monster, as Julian pulls into the parking lot and for some reason he's passed the hotel twice and I keep asking him why and he keeps asking me if I really want to go through with this and I keep telling him that I do. As soon as I step out of the car, I look at the pool and wonder if anybody has drowned in the pool. The Saint Marquis is a hollow hotel; it has a swimming pool in a courtyard surrounded by rooms. There's a fat man in a lounge chair, his body shining, suntan oil slathered onto it. He stares at the two of us as we walk toward the room Finn told Julian to go to. The man's staying in room 001. Julian walks up to the door and knocks. The curtains are closed and a face, a shadow, peers out. The door's opened by a man, forty, forty-five, wearing slacks and a shirt and a tie, who asks, 'Yes . . . what may I do for you?'

'You're Mr. Erickson, right?'

'Yes . . . Oh, you must be . . .' His voice trails off as he looks Julian and me over.

'Is something wrong?' Julian asks.

'No, not at all. Why don't you two come in?'

'Thanks,' Julian says.

I follow Julian into the room and become unnerved. I hate hotel rooms. My great-grandfather died in one. At the Stardust in Las Vegas. He had been dead two days before anybody found him.

'Would you boys like a drink?' the man asks.

I have a feeling that these men always ask this and though I want one, badly, I look at Julian, who shakes his head and says, 'No, thank you, sir.' And I also say, 'No, thank you, sir.'

'Why don't you two boys make yourself comfortable and sit down.'

'Can I take my jacket off?' Julian asks.

'Yes. By all means, son.'

The man begins to make himself a drink.

'Are you in L.A. for long?' Julian asks.

'No, no, just a week, for business.' The man sips his drink.

'What do you do?'

'I'm into real estate, son.'

I look over at Julian and wonder if this man knows my father. I look down and realize that I don't have anything to say, but I try to think of something; the need to hear my own voice begins to get more intense and I keep wondering if my father knows this guy. I try to shake the thought from my head, the idea of this guy maybe coming up to my father at Ma Maison or Trumps, but it stays there, stuck.

Julian speaks up. 'Where are you from?'

'Indiana.'

'Oh, really? Where in Indiana?'

'Muncie.'

'Oh. Muncie, Indiana.'

'That's right.'

There's a pause and the man shifts his eyes from Julian to me and then back to Julian. He sips his drink.

'Well, which of you young men would like to get up?' The man from Indiana is gripping his glass too tightly and he sets his drink on the bar. Julian stands up.

The man nods, and asks, 'Why don't you take off your tie?'

Julian does.

The man shifts his gaze from Julian over to me, to make sure that I'm watching.

'And your shoes and socks.'

Julian does this also and then looks down.

'And . . . uh, the rest.'

Julian slips out of his shirt and pants and the man peels back the window shade and looks out onto Sunset Boulevard and then back at Julian.

'Do you like living in L.A.?'

'Yeah. I love L.A.,' Julian says, folding his pants.

The man looks over at me and then says, 'Oh no, this won't do. Why don't you sit over there, near the window. That's better.' The man sits me down in an easy chair and positions me nearer the bed and then, satisfied, walks up to Julian and places his hand on Julian's bare shoulder. His hand drops down to Julian's jockey shorts and Julian closes his eyes.

'You're a very nice young man.'

An image of Julian in fifth grade, kicking a soccer ball across a green field.

'Yes, you're a very beautiful boy,' the man from Indiana says, 'and here, that's all that matters.'

Julian opens his eyes and stares into mine and I turn away and notice a fly buzzing lazily over to the wall next to the bed. I wonder what the man and Julian are going to do. I tell myself I could leave. I could simply say to the man from Muncie and Julian that I want to leave. But, again, the words don't, can't, come out and I sit there and the need to see the worst washes over me, quickly, eagerly.

The man walks over to the bathroom and tells us both

that he'll be out in a minute. He closes the bathroom door. I get up from the chair and walk over to the bar to look for something to drink. I notice the man's wallet which he left on the bar and I look through it. I'm so nervous I don't care, don't even know why I'm doing it. There are a lot of business cards in it but I don't look at any, not wanting to see my father's. There are some credit cards and the usual amount of cash someone from out of town might carry when coming into the city. There are also pictures of a very tired, pretty woman, the man's wife probably, and two pictures of his children, all boys, straight-limbed, and with short blond hair and striped shirts, looking full of confidence. The pictures depress me and I put the wallet back down on the bar and wonder if the man took the pictures. I look over at Julian, who's sitting on the edge of the bed, head down. I sit down and then lean over and turn the stereo on.

The man comes out of the bathroom and tells me, 'No. No music. I want you to hear it all. Everything.' He switches the stereo off. I ask the man if I can use the bathroom. Julian takes off his underwear. The man smiles for some reason and says yes and I walk into the bathroom and lock the door and turn on both faucets in the sink and flush the toilet repeatedly as I try to throw up, but I don't. I wipe my mouth and then come back into the room. The sun's shifting, shadows stretching across the walls, and Julian's trying to smile. The man's smiling back, the shadows stretching across his face.

I light a cigarette.

The man rolls Julian over.

Wonder if he's for sale.

I don't close my eyes.

You can disappear here without knowing it.

Julian and I walk out into the parking lot. We've been in the hotel room since four o'clock and it's now nine. I have been sitting in the chair for five hours. As we get into Julian's car, I ask him where we're going.

'To The Land's End to get your money. You want your money, don't you?' he asks. 'Don't you, Clay?'

I look at Julian's face and remember mornings sitting in his Porsche, double-parked, smoking thinly rolled joints, listening to the new Squeeze album before classes started at nine, and even though the image comes back to me, it doesn't disturb me anymore. Julian's face looks older to me now.

It's around ten and The Land's End is crowded. The club lies on Hollywood Boulevard and Julian parks in back, in an alley, and I walk with him up to the entrance and Julian pushes his way through the line and kids jeer, but Julian ignores them. From the back door you walk into the club like you're walking into a cellar and it's dark and like a cave with all these partitions separating the club into small areas where groups huddle in the darkness. As we walk in, the manager, who looks like a fifty-year-old surfer, is hassling with a group of teenagers who are trymg to get in and who are obviously underage. And as the manager winks at Julian and lets us both through, one of the girls in line stares at me and smiles, her wet lips, covered with this pink garish lipstick, part and she bares her upper teeth like she was some sort of dog or wolf, growling, about to attack, and she knows Julian and she says something rude that I can't hear and Julian gives her the finger.

Before I can make out any faces, my eyes have to wait a minute to get used to the darkness. The club's crowded tonight and some of the kids waiting out in back won't be able to get in. 'Tainted Love' is playing, loudly, over the stereo system and the dance floor is packed with people, most of them young, most of them bored, trying to look turned on. There are some guys sitting at tables who all look at this one gorgeous girl, longingly, hoping for at least one dance or a blow job in Daddy's car and there are all these girls, looking indifferent or bored, smoking clove cigarettes, all of them or at least most of them staring at one blond-haired boy standing in the back with sunglasses on. Julian recognizes the guy and tells me that he works for Finn also.

We pass through the crowd and walk into the back, leaving the thumping music and the smoke-filled room behind us. In the back and up the stairs is where Lee, the newly appointed part-time DJ, hangs out. Finn's sitting on a couch talking to him and it seems that it's Lee's first night and Lee, blond and tan, seems nervous. Finn introduces Julian and me to Lee and then asks Julian how everything went and Julian mutters fine and tells Finn that he wants the money. Finn tells him that he'll give it to him, to both of us, at Eddie's party; that he wants Julian

to do a little favor for him; after the little favor, Finn says
that he'll be more than happy to give us our money.

Though Lee's eighteen, he looks a lot younger than
Julian or I and this scares me. Lee's office looks over
Hollywood Boulevard and, as Julian sighs and turns away
from Finn, who starts to talk to Lee, I walk to the window
and stare at the cars. An ambulance passes by. Then a
police siren. Lee looks very preppy, is what Finn says, and
then something like, 'They like that. That preppy look.' It
seems that Lee's ready and so is Finn and Lee says that
he's a little nervous and Finn laughs and says, 'There's
nothing to worry about. You don't have to do that much.
Not with these guys. Just typical studio execs, that's all.'
Finn smiles and straightens Lee's tie. 'And if you have to
do anything . . . well, hey, you make the money, babes.'
And Julian says, 'Bullshit' a little too loudly and Finn says,
'Watch it' and I don't know what I'm doing here and I
look over at Lee, who's smiling dumbly, and do and don't
see Julian in the same innocent smile.

Julian follows Finn and Lee in Finn's Rolls-Royce and
Julian tells them at a stoplight that he has to drop me off
at my car so that I can follow them to Eddie's place. Julian
drops me back at my car at the arcade in Westwood and
then I follow the two cars up into the hills.

The house I follow Finn and Lee and Julian to is in Bel
Air and it's a huge stone house with a sprawling front lawn

and Spanish fountains and gargoyles looming up above the roof. The house is on Bellagio and I wonder what Bellagio means as I pull into the wide, circular driveway and a valet attendant opens the door and as I get out of the car I can see Finn wrapping his arms around Julian and Lee and they walk through the open front door before me. I follow them into the house and there are mostly men inside, but there are some women too and everyone seems to recognize Finn. Some people even recognize Julian. There's a strobe light on in the living room and for a moment the slight edginess I feel turns into a sort of wild dizziness and my knees almost buckle and it seems that everyone's talking, eyes constantly searching; beat of the music matching the movements and the stares.

'Hey, Finn, my main man, how've you been?'

'Hey, Bobby. Great. How's business?'

'Fab. And who's this?'

'This is my best boy. Julian. And this is Lee.'

'Hey,' Bobby says.

'Hi,' Lee says, and smiles, looks down.

'Say hello.' Finn nudges Julian.

'Hello.'

'Wanna dance?'

Finn nudges Julian again.

'No, not now. Could you excuse me?' Julian breaks away from Finn and Lee and Finn calls after him and I follow Julian through the crowd, but I lose him and so I light a cigarette and wander over to the bathroom, but it's locked. The Clash are singing 'Somebody Got Murdered' and I lean against the wall and break out into a cold sweat and there's a young guy who I sort of recognize sitting in a chair staring at me from across the room and I stare back, confused, wondering if he knows me, but I realize it's pointless. That the guy is stoned and doesn't see me, doesn't see anything.

The bathroom door opens and a man and a woman come out together, laughing, and they pass me and I go in and shut the door and open a small vial and notice that I don't have too much coke left, but I do what's left of it and I take a drink from the faucet and look at myself in the mirror, run my hand over my hair, and then across my cheek, decide I need to shave. Suddenly Julian bursts in, along with Finn. Finn smashes him against the wall and locks the bathroom door.

'What in the hell are you doing?'

'Nothing,' Julian yells. 'Nothing. Just leave me alone. I'm going home. Give Clay his money.'

'You're acting like a real asshole and I want it stopped. I have some very important clients out there tonight and you are not going to fuck it up.'

'Leave me the fuck alone,' Julian says. 'Don't touch me.'

I lean up against the wall and look down at the floor.

Finn looks at me and then at Julian and sneers. 'Jesus, Julian, you are really pathetic, man. What are you gonna do? You don't have any choice. Do you understand that? You can't leave. You can't walk out now. Are you gonna run to Mommy or Daddy, huh?'

'Stop it.'

'Your expensive shrink?'

'Stop it, Finn.'

'Who? Do you have any friends left? What the fuck are you gonna do? Just leave?'

'Stop it,' Julian screams.

'You come to me a year ago with a huge debt to some dealers and I give you a job and show you off and take you around and I give you all these clothes and all the fuckin' coke you could snort, and what do you do in return?'

'I know. Shut up,' Julian screams, choking, covering his head with his hands.

'You act like an arrogant, selfish, ungrateful—'

'Fuck off, you—'

'—little prick.'

'—asshole pimp.'

'Don't you appreciate what I've done for you?' Finn pushes Julian harder against the door. 'Huh? Don't you?'

'Stop it, you asshole pimp.'

'Don't you? Answer me. Don't you?'

'Done for me? You've turned me into a whore.' Julian's face is all red and his eyes are wet and I'm freaking out, just trying to stare at the floor whenever Julian or Finn looks over at me.

'No. I haven't done that, man,' Finn says quietly.

'What?'

'I didn't turn you into a whore. You did it yourself.'

The music's pumping through the walls and I can actually feel it vibrate against my back, almost through me, and Julian's still looking down and he tries to move or turn away but Finn holds his shoulders back and Julian starts to laugh-cry softly and he tells Finn that he's sorry.

'I can't do it anymore . . . Please, Finn . . .'

'Sorry, babe, I just can't let you go that easily.'

Julian slowly falls to the floor in a sitting position.

Finn has taken out a syringe and a spoon and a book of matches from Le Dome.

'What are you doing?' Julian sniffs.

'My best boy has got to cool down tonight.'

'Finn . . . But I'm leaving.' Julian starts to laugh. 'I really am. I've paid my fucking debt. No more. This is it.'

But Finn isn't listening and he squats down and grabs Julian's arm and pushes back the jacket sleeve and the shirt and he takes off his own belt and ties it around the arm and slaps at his arm to find a vein and gets one after a while and while he's heating up something in the deep, silver spoon all Julian keeps saying is 'Finn. Don't.' Finn jabs the needle into Julian's arm and jiggles it.

'What are you gonna do? You have nowhere to go. You going to tell everyone? That you whored yourself to pay off a drug debt? Man, you are more naive than I thought. But come on, baby, you'll feel better.'

Disappear Here.

The syringe fills with blood.

You're a beautiful boy and that's all that matters.

Wonder if he's for sale.

People are afraid to merge. To merge.

Finn finally leads Julian out of the bathroom and I follow them and Finn begins to lead Julian up the stairs and, as the two of them make their way up the long staircase, I can see that there's a door open just a crack at the top of the stairs and the music stops for a minute and I can hear low moans coming from the room, and as Finn leads Julian into the room, a scream suddenly bursts out, and Julian disappears with Finn and the door slams shut. I turn away and leave the house.

After I leave the party, I head for The Roxy, where X is playing. It's almost midnight and The Roxy is crowded and I find Trent standing near the entrance and he asks me where I've been and I don't say anything and then he hands me a drink. It's hot in the club and I hold the drink up to my forehead, my face. Trent mentions that Rip's here and I walk with Trent over to where Rip is, and Trent tells me that they're going to be singing 'Sex and Dying in High Society' any minute now and I say 'That's great.' Rip's wearing black 501s and a white X T-shirt and Spin's wearing a T-shirt that reads: 'Gumby. Pokey. The Block-heads' and black 501s also. Rip comes up to me and the first thing he says is, 'There are too many fucking Mexicans here, dude.'

Spin snorts and says, 'Let's kill 'em all.'

Trent must think that this is a pretty good idea because he laughs and nods.

Rip glances at me and says, 'Jesus, dude. You look real bad. What's wrong? Want some coke?'

I manage to actually shake my head and finish Trent's drink.

A dark boy with a thin mustache and an 'Under The Big Black Sun' T-shirt bumps into me and Rip grabs his shoulders and pushes him back into the dancing crowd and shouts 'Fuckin' Spic!'

Spin's talking to somebody named Ross, and Spin turns to Rip after Rip's turned away from the stage.

'Listen, Ross has found something in the alley behind Flip.'

'What?' Rip shouts, interested.

'A body.'

'You kidding me?'

Ross shakes his head nervously, smiling.

'This, I've got to see.' Rip grins. 'Come on, Clay.'

'No,' I say. 'I don't think so. I want to see the show.'

'Come on. I want to show you something at my place anyway.'

Trent and I follow Rip and Spin to Rip's car and Rip tells us to meet them in back of Flip. Trent and I drive down Melrose and Flip is all lit up and closed and we all make a left and then park behind the building in the deserted lot in back. Ross gets out of his VW Rabbit and motions for Rip and Spin and me and Trent to follow him to the alley behind the empty store.

'I hope nobody told the police,' Ross mutters.

'Who else knows about this?' Rip asks.

'Some friends of mine. They found him this afternoon.'

Two girls come out of the darkness of the alley, giggling and holding onto each other. One says, 'Jesus, Ross, who is that guy?'

'I don't know, Alicia.'

'What happened to him?'

'O.D.'d, I guess.'

'Have you called the police?'

'What for?'

One of the girls says, 'We gotta bring Marcia. She'll freak out.'

'Have you girls seen Mimi?' Ross asks.

'She was over here with Derf and they left. We're gonna see X over at The Roxy.'

'We were just there.'

'Oh, how are they?'

'Okay. They didn't sing "Adult Books" though.'

'They didn't?'

'Nope.'

'Oh, they never do.'

'I know.'

'Bummer.'

The girls leave, talking about Billy Zoom, and Rip and Spin and Trent and I follow Ross deeper into the alley.

He's lying against the back wall, propped up. The face is bloated and pale and the eyes are shut, mouth open and the face belongs to some young, eighteen-, nineteen-year-old boy, dried blood, crusted, above the upper lip.

'Jesus,' Rip says.

Spin's eyes are wide.

Trent just stands there and says something like 'Wild.'

Rip jabs the boy in the stomach with his foot.

'Sure he's dead?'

'See him moving?' Ross giggles.

'Christ, man. Where did you find this?' Spin asks.

'Word gets around.'

I cannot take my eyes off the dead boy. There are moths flying above his head, twirling around the light bulb that hangs over him, illuminating the scene. Spin kneels down and looks into the boy's face and studies it earnestly. Trent starts to laugh and lights up a joint. Ross is leaning against a wall, smoking, and he offers me a cigarette. I shake my head and light my own, but my hand's shaking badly and I drop it.

'Look at that, no socks,' Trent mutters.

We stand there for a while longer. A wind comes through the alley. Sounds of traffic can be heard coming from Melrose.

'Wait a minute,' Spin says. 'I think I know this guy.'

'Bullshit,' Rip laughs.

'Man, you are so sick,' Trent says, handing me the joint.

I take a drag and hand it back to Trent and wonder about what would happen if the boy's eyes were to open.

'Let's get out of here,' Ross says.

'Wait.' Rip motions for him to stay and then sticks a cigarette in the boy's mouth. We stand there for five more minutes. Then Spin stands up and shakes his head, scratches at Gumby, and says, 'Man, I need a cigarette.'

Rip gets up and holds onto my arm and says to me and Trent, 'Listen, you two, you've gotta come over to my place.'

'Why?' I ask.

'I've got something at my place that will blow your mind.'

Trent giggles expectantly and we all leave the alley.

When we get to Rip's apartment on Wilshire, he leads us into the bedroom. There's a naked girl, really young and pretty, lying on the mattress. Her legs are spread and tied to the bedposts and her arms are tied above her head. Her cunt is all rashed and looks dry and I can see that it's been shaved. She keeps moaning and murmuring words and moving her head from side to side, her eyes half-closed. Someone's put a lot of makeup on her, clumsily, and she keeps licking her lips, her tongue drags slowly, repeatedly, across them. Spin kneels by the bed and picks up a syringe and whispers something into her ear. The girl doesn't open her eyes. Spin digs the syringe into her arm. I just stare. Trent says 'Wow.' Rip says something.

'She's twelve.'

'And she is tight, man,' Spin laughs.

'Who is she?' I ask.

'Her name is Shandra and she goes to Corvalis' is all Rip says.

Ross is playing Centipede in the living room and the sound of the video game carries to where we're standing. Spin puts a tape on and then takes off his shirt and then his jeans. He has a hard-on and he pushes it at the girl's lips and then looks over at us. 'You can watch if you want.'

I leave the room.

Rip follows me.

'Why?' is all I ask Rip.

'What?'

'Why, Rip?'

Rip looks confused. 'Why that? You mean in there?'

I try to nod.

'Why not? What the hell?'

'Oh God, Rip, come on, she's eleven.'

'Twelve,' Rip corrects.

'Yeah, twelve,' I say, thinking about it for a moment.

'Hey, don't look at me like I'm some sort of scumbag or something. I'm not.'

'It's . . .' my voice trails off.

'It's what?' Rip wants to know.

'It's . . . I don't think it's right.'

'What's right? If you want something, you have the right to take it. If you want to do something, you have the right to do it.'

I lean up against the wall. I can hear Spin moaning in the bedroom and then the sound of a hand slapping maybe a face.

'But you don't need anything. You have everything,' I tell him.

Rip looks at me. 'No. I don't.'

'What?'

'No, I don't.'

There's a pause and then I ask, 'Oh, shit, Rip, what don't you have?'

'I don't have anything to lose.'

Rip turns away and walks back into the bedroom. I look in and Trent's already unbuttoning his shirt, staring at Spin, who's straddling the girl's head. 'Come on, Trent,' I say. 'Let's get outta here.'

He looks over at me and then at Spin and the girl and says, 'I think I'm gonna stay.'

I just stand there. Spin turns his head while he's thrusting into the girl's head and says, 'Shut the door if you're gonna stay. Okay?'

'You should stay,' Trent says.

I close the door and walk away and through the living room, where Ross is still playing Centipede.

'I got the high score,' he says. He notices that I'm leaving and asks, 'Hey, where are you going?'

I don't say anything.

'I bet you're gonna check out that body again, right?'

I close the door behind me.

A few miles from Rancho Mirage, there was a house that belonged to a friend of one of my cousins. He was blond and good-looking and was going to go to Stanford in the fall and he came from a good family from San Francisco. He would come down to Palm Springs on weekends and have these parties in the house in the desert. Kids from L.A. and San Francisco and Sacramento would come down for the weekend and stay for the party. One night, near the end of summer, there was a party that somehow got out of hand. A young girl from San Diego who had been at the party had been found the next morning, her wrists and ankles tied together. She had been raped repeatedly. She also had been strangled and her throat had been slit and her breasts had been cut off and someone had stuck candles where they used to be. Her body had been found at the Sun Air Drive-In hanging upside down from the swing set that lay near the corner of the parking lot. And the friend of my cousin disappeared. Some say he went to Mexico and some say he went to Canada or London. Most people say he went to Mexico, though. The mother was put in an institution and the house lay empty for two years. Then one night it burned down and a lot of people say that the guy came back from Mexico, or London, or Canada, and burned it down.

I drive up the canyon road where the house used to be, still wearing the same clothes I had on earlier that afternoon, in Finn's office, in the hotel room of the Saint Marquis, behind Flip, in the alley, and I park the car and sit there, smoking, looking for a shadow or figure lurking behind the rocks. I cock my head and listen for a murmur or a whisper. Some people say you can see the boy walking through the canyons at night, peering out over the desert, wandering through the ruins of the house. Some also say that the police caught him and put him away. In Camarillo, hundreds of miles from Palo Alto and Stanford.

I remember this story clearly as I drive away from the ruins of the house and I begin to drive even farther out into the desert. The night's warm and the weather reminds me of nights in Palm Springs when my mother and father would have friends over and play bridge and I would take my father's car and put the top down and drive through the desert listening to The Eagles or Fleetwood Mac, the hot wind blowing through my hair.

And I remember the mornings when I would be the first one up and I would watch the steam rise off the heated pool on the cold desert at dawn, my mother sitting in the sun all day when it was so quiet and still that I could see the shadows caused by the sun move and shift across the bottom of the still pool and my mother's dark, tan back.

The week before I leave, one of my sister's cats disappears. It's a small brown kitten and my sister says that last night she could hear squealings and a yelp. There are pieces of matted fur and dried blood near the side door. A lot of cats in the neighborhood have had to be kept inside because, if they're allowed out at night, there's a chance that the coyotes will eat them. On some nights when the moon's full and the sky's clear, I look outside and I can see shapes moving through the streets, through the canyons. I used to mistake them for large, misshaped dogs. It was only later I realized they were coyotes. On some nights, late, I've been driving across Mulholland and have had to swerve and stop suddenly and in the glare of the headlights I've seen coyotes running slowly through the fog with red rags in their mouths and it's only when I come home that I realize that the red rag is a cat. It's something one must live with if you live in the hills.

Written on the bathroom wall at Pages, below where it says 'Julian gives great head. And is dead.': 'Fuck you Mom and Dad. You suck cunt. You suck cock. You both can die because that's what you did to me. You left me to die. You both are so fucking hopeless. Your daughter is an Iranian and your son is a faggot. You both can rot in fucking shitting asshole hell. Burn, you fucking dumbshits. Burn, fuckers. Burn.'

The week before I leave, I listen to a song by an L.A. composer about the city. I would listen to the song over and over, ignoring the rest of the album. It wasn't that I liked the song so much; it was more that it confused me and I would try to decipher it. For instance, I wanted to know why the bum in the song was on his knees. Someone told me that the bum was so grateful to be in the city instead of somewhere else. I told this person that I thought he missed the point and the person told me, in a tone I found slightly conspiratorial, 'No, dude . . . I don't think so.'

I sat in my room a lot, the week before I left, watching a television show that was on in the afternoons and that played videos while a DJ from a local rock station introduced the clips. There would be about a hundred teenagers dancing in front of a huge screen on which the videos were played; the images dwarfing the teenagers – and I would recognize people whom I had seen at clubs, dancing on the show, smiling for the cameras, and then turning and looking up to the lighted, monolithic screen that was flashing the images at them. Some of them would mouth the words to the song that was being played. But

I'd concentrate on the teenagers who didn't mouth the words; the teenagers who had forgotten them; the teenagers who maybe never knew them.

Rip and I were driving on Mulholland one day before I left and Rip was chewing on a plastic eyeball and wearing a Billy Idol T-shirt and kept flashing the eyeball between his lips. I kept trying to smile and Rip mentioned something about going to Palm Springs one night before I left and I nodded, giving in to the heat. On one of Mulholland's most treacherous turns, Rip slowed the car down and parked it on the edge of the road and got out and motioned for me to do so too. I followed him to where he stood. He pointed out the number of wrecked cars at the bottom of the hill. Some were rusted and burnt, some new and crushed, their bright colors almost obscene in the glittering sunshine. I tried to count the cars; there must have been twenty or thirty cars down there. Rip told me about friends of his who died on that curve; people who misunderstood the road. People who made a mistake late in the night and who sailed off into nothingness. Rip told me that, on some quiet nights, late, you can hear the screeching of tires and then a long silence; a whoosh and then, barely audible, an impact. And sometimes, if one listens very carefully, there are screams in the night that can't last too long. Rip said he doubted that they'll ever get the cars out of there, that they'll probably wait until it gets full of cars and use it as an example and then bury it.

And standing there on the hill, overlooking the smog-soaked, baking Valley and feeling the hot winds returning and the dust swirling at my feet and the sun, gigantic, a ball of fire, rising over it, I believed him. And later when we got into the car he took a turn down a street that I was pretty sure was a dead end.

'Where are we going?' I asked.

'I don't know,' he said. 'Just driving.'

'But this road doesn't go anywhere,' I told him.

'That doesn't matter.'

'What does?' I asked, after a little while.

'Just that we're on it, dude,' he said.

Before I left, a woman had her throat slit and was thrown from a moving car in Venice; a series of fires raged out of control in Chatsworth, the work of an arsonist; a man in Encino killed his wife and two children. Four teenagers, none of whom I knew, died in a car accident on Pacific Coast Highway. Muriel was readmitted to Cedars-Sinai. A guy, nicknamed Conan, killed himself at a fraternity party at U.C.L.A. And I met Alana accidentally in The Beverly Center.

'I haven't seen you around,' I told her.

'Yeah, well, I haven't been around too much.'

'I met someone who knows you.'

'Who?'

'Evan Dickson. Do you know him?'

'I'm going-out with him.'

'Yeah, I know. That's what he told me.'

'But he's fucking this guy named Derf, who goes to Buckley.'

'Oh.'

'Yeah, oh,' she said.

'So what?'

'It's just so typical.'

'Yes,' I told her. 'It is.'

'Did you have a good time while you were here?'

'No.'

'That's too bad.'

And I see Finn at the Hughes Market on Doheny on Tuesday afternoon. It's hot and I've been lying out by the pool all day. I get in my car and take my sisters to the market. They haven't gone to school today and they're wearing shorts and T-shirts and sunglasses and I'm wearing an old Polo bathing suit and a T-shirt. Finn is with Jared and he notices me in the frozen foods section. He's wearing sandals and a Hard Rock Cafe T-shirt and he glances at me once and then looks down and then looks back up. I turn away quickly and walk to the vegetables. He follows me. I pick up a six-pack of iced tea and then a carton of cigarettes. I look back at him and our eyes meet and he grins and I turn away. He follows me to the checkstand.

'Hey, Clay.' He winks.

'Hi,' I say, smiling, walking away.

'Catch ya later,' he says, cocking his fingers as if they were a gun.

The last week. I'm in Parachute with Trent. Trent tries on clothes. I lean against a wall, reading an old issue of *Interview*. Some pretty blond-haired boy, I think it's Evan, is trying on clothes. He doesn't go into a booth to try them on. He tries them on in the middle of the store in front of a full-length mirror. He looks at himself as he stands there with only his jockey shorts and argyle socks on. The boy's broken from his trance when his boyfriend, also blond and pretty, comes up behind him and squeezes his neck. Then he tries something else on. Trent tells me that he saw the boy with Julian parked in Julian's black Porsche outside of Beverly Hills High, talking to a kid who looked about fourteen. Trent tells me that even though Julian was wearing sunglasses, he could still see the purple bruises around his eyes.

While reading the paper at twilight by the pool, I see a story about how a local man tried to bury himself alive in his backyard because it was 'so hot, too hot.' I read the article a second time and then put the paper down and watch my sisters. They're still wearing their bikinis and sunglasses and they lie beneath the darkening sky and play a game in which they pretend to be dead. They ask me to judge which one of them can look dead the longest; the one who wins gets to push the other one into the pool. I watch them and listen to the tape that's playing on the Walkman I'm wearing. The Go-Go's are singing '*I wanna be worlds away / I know things will be okay when I get worlds away.*' Whoever made the tape then let the record skip and I close my eyes and hear them start to sing 'Vacation' and when I open my eyes, my sisters are floating face down in the pool, wondering who can look drowned the longest.

I go to the movies with Trent. The theater we go to in Westwood is almost empty except for a few scattered people, most of them sitting alone. I see an old friend from high school sitting with some pretty blond girl near the front, on the aisle, but I don't say anything and I'm kind of relieved when the lights go down that Trent hasn't recognized him. Later, in the video arcade, Trent plays a game called Burger Time in which there are all these video hot dogs and eggs that chase around a short, bearded chef and Trent wants to teach me how to play, but I don't want to. I just keep staring at the maniacal, wiggling hot dogs and for some reason it's just too much to take and I walk away, looking for something else to play. But all the games seem to deal with beetles and bees and moths and snakes and mosquitoes and frogs drowning and mad spiders eating large purple video flies and the music that goes along with the games makes me feel dizzy and gives me a headache and the images are hard to shake off, even after I leave the arcade.

On the way home, Trent tells me, 'Well, you really acted like a dick today.' On Beverly Glen I'm behind a red Jaguar with a license plate that reads DECLINE and I have to pull over.

'What's wrong, Clay?' Trent asks me, this edge in his voice.

'Nothing,' I manage to say.

'What in the fuck is wrong with you?'

I tell him I have a headache and drive him home and tell him I'll call him from New Hampshire.

For some reason I remember standing in a phone booth at a 76 Station in Palm Desert at nine-thirty on a Sunday night, late last August, waiting for a phone call from Blair, who was leaving for New York the next morning for three weeks to join her father on location. I was wearing jeans and a T-shirt and an old baggy argyle sweater and tennis shoes with no socks and my hair was unbrushed and I was smoking a cigarette. And from where I was standing, I could see a bus stop with four or five people sitting or standing under the fluorescent street lights, waiting. There was a teenage boy, maybe fifteen, sixteen, who I thought was hitchhiking and I was feeling on edge and I wanted to tell the boy something, but the bus came and the boy got on. I was waiting in a phone booth with no door and the Day-

*Glo light was insistent and giving me a headache. A parade
of ants marched across an empty yogurt cup that I put my
cigarette out into. It was strange that night. There were
three phone booths at this particular gas station on that
Sunday night last August and each booth was being used.
There was a young surfer in the booth next to mine in OP
shorts and a yellow T-shirt with 'MAUI' etched across it
and I was pretty sure that he was waiting for the bus. I
didn't think the surfer was talking to anyone; that he was
pretending to be talking and that there was no one listening
on the other end and all I could keep thinking about was is
it better to pretend to talk than not talk at all and I kept
remembering this night at Disneyland with Blair. The surfer
kept looking over at me and I kept turning away, waiting
for the phone to ring. A car pulled up with a license plate
that read 'GABSTOY' and a girl with a black Joan Jett
haircut, probably Gabs, and her boyfriend, who was wearing a black Clash T-shirt, got out of the car, motor still
running, and I could hear the strains of an old Squeeze
song. I finished another cigarette and lit one more. Some of
the ants were drowning in the yogurt. The bus came by.
People got on. Nobody got off. And I kept thinking about
that night at Disneyland and thinking about New Hampshire and about Blair and me breaking up.*

*A warm wind whipped through the empty gas station
and the surfer, who I thought was a hustler, hung up the
phone and I heard no dime drop and pretended not to
notice. He got on a bus that passed by. GABSTOY left. The
phone rang. It was Blair. And I told her not to go. She
asked me where I was. I told her that I was in a phone
booth in Palm Desert. She asked 'Why?' I asked 'Why not?'*

I told her not to go to New York. She said that it was a little too late to be bringing this up. I told her to come to Palm Springs with me. She told me that I hurt her; that I promised I was going to stay in L.A.; that I promised I would never go back East. I told her that I was sorry and that things will be all right and she said that she had heard that already from me and that if we really like each other, what difference will four months make. I asked her if she remembered that night at Disneyland and she asked, 'What night at Disneyland?' and we hung up.

And so I drove back to L.A. and went to a movie and sat by myself and then drove around until one or so and sat in a restaurant on Sunset and drank coffee and finished my cigarettes and stayed until they closed. And I drove home and Blair called me. I told her that I'll miss her and that maybe when I get back, things will work out. She said maybe, and then that she did remember that night at Disneyland. I left for New Hampshire the next week and didn't talk to her for four months.

Before I leave I meet Blair for lunch. She's sitting on the terrace of The Old World on Sunset waiting for me. She's wearing sunglasses and sipping a glass of white wine she probably got with her fake I.D. Maybe the waiter didn't even ask her, I think to myself as I walk in through the front door. I tell the hostess that I'm with the girl sitting on the terrace. She's sitting alone and she turns her head toward the breeze and that one moment suggests to me a move on her part of some sort of confidence, or some sort of courage and I'm envious. She doesn't see me as I come up behind her and kiss her on the cheek. She smiles and turns around and lowers her sunglasses and she smells like wine and lipstick and perfume and I sit down and leaf through the menu. I put the menu down and watch the cars pass by, starting to think that maybe this is a mistake.

'I'm surprised you came,' she says.

'Why? I told you I was going to come.'

'Yes, you did,' she murmurs. 'Where have you been?'

'I had an early lunch with my father.'

'That must have been nice.' I wonder if she's being sarcastic.

'Yeah,' I say, unsure. I light a cigarette.

'What else have you been doing?'

'Why?'

'Come on, don't get so pissed off. I only want to talk.'

'So talk.' I squint as smoke from the cigarette floats into my eyes.

'Listen.' She sips her wine. 'Tell me about your weekend.'

I sigh, actually surprised that I don't remember too much of what happened. 'I don't remember. Nothing.'

'Oh.'

I pick up the menu again and then put it down without opening it.

'So, you're actually going back to school,' she says.

'I guess so. There's nothing here.'

'Did you expect to find something?'

'I don't know. I've been here a long time.'

Like I've been here for ever.

I quietly kick my foot against the terrace railing and ignore her. It is a mistake. Suddenly she looks at me and takes off her Wayfarers.

'Clay, did you ever love me?'

I'm studying a billboard and say that I didn't hear what she said.

'I asked if you ever loved me?'

On the terrace the sun bursts into my eyes and for one blinding moment I see myself clearly. I remember the first time we made love, in the house in Palm Springs, her body tan and wet, lying against cool, white sheets.

'Don't do this, Blair,' I tell her.

'Just tell me.'

I don't say anything.

'Is it such a hard question to answer?'

I look at her straight on.

'Yes or no?'

'Why?'

'Dammit, Clay,' she sighs.

'Yeah, sure, I guess.'

'Don't lie to me.'

'What in the fuck do you want to hear?'

'Just tell me,' she says, her voice rising.

'No,' I almost shout. 'I never did.' I almost start to laugh.

She draws in a breath and says, 'Thank you. That's all I wanted to know.' She sips her wine.

'Did you ever love me?' I ask her back, though by now I can't even care.

She pauses. 'I thought about it and yeah, I did once. I mean I really did. Everything was all right for a while. You were kind.' She looks down and then goes on. 'But it was like you weren't there. Oh shit, this isn't going to make any sense.' She stops.

I look at her, waiting for her to go on, looking up at the billboard. Disappear Here.

'I don't know if any other person I've been with has been really there, either . . . but at least they tried.'

I finger the menu; put my cigarette out.

'You never did. Other people made an effort and you just . . . It was just beyond you.' She takes another sip of her wine. 'You were never there. I felt sorry for you for a little while, but then I found it hard to. You're a beautiful boy, Clay, but that's about it.'

I watch the cars pass by on Sunset.

'It's hard to feel sorry for someone who doesn't care.'

'Yeah?' I ask.

'What do you care about? What makes you happy?'

'Nothing. Nothing makes me happy. I like nothing,' I tell her.

'Did you ever care about me, Clay?'

I don't say anything, look back at the menu.

'Did you ever care about me?' she asks again.

'I don't want to care. If I care about things, it'll just be worse, it'll just be another thing to worry about. It's less painful if I don't care.'

'I cared about you for a little while.'

I don't say anything.

She takes off her sunglasses and finally says, 'I'll see you later, Clay.' She gets up.

'Where are you going?' I suddenly don't want to leave Blair here. I almost want to take her back with me.

'Have to meet someone for lunch.'

'But what about us?'

'What about us?' She stands there for a moment, waiting. I keep staring at the billboard until it begins to blur and when my vision becomes clearer I watch as Blair's car glides out of the parking lot and becomes lost in the haze of traffic on Sunset. The waiter comes over and asks, 'Is everything okay, sir?'

I look up and put on my sunglasses and try to smile. 'Yeah.'

Blair calls me the night before I leave.

'Don't go,' she says.

'I'll only be gone a couple of months.'

'That's a long time.'

'There's always summer.'

'That's a long time.'

'I'll be back. It's not that long.'

'Shit, Clay.'

'You've got to believe me.'

'I don't.'

'You have to.'

'You're lying.'

'No, I'm not.'

And before I left, I read an article in *Los Angeles Magazine* about a street called Sierra Bonita in Hollywood. A

street I'd driven along many times. The article said that
there were people who drove on the street and saw ghosts;
apparitions of the Wild West. I read that Indians dressed
in nothing but loincloths and on horseback were spotted,
and that one man had a tomahawk, which disappeared
seconds later, thrown through his open window. One
elderly couple said that an Indian appeared in their living
room on Sierra Bonita, moaning incantations. A man had
crashed into a palm tree because he had seen a covered
wagon in his path and it forced him to swerve.

When I left there was nothing much in my room except
a couple of books, the television, stereo, the mattress, the
Elvis Costello poster, eyes still staring out the window; the
shoebox with the pictures of Blair in the closet. There was
also a poster of California that I had pinned up onto my
wall. One of the pins had fallen out and the poster was
old and torn down the middle and was tilted and hanging
unevenly from the wall.

I drove out to Topanga Canyon that night and parked
near an old deserted carnival that still stood, alone in a
valley, empty, quiet. From where I was I could hear the
wind moving through the canyons. The ferris wheel
pitched slightly. A coyote howled. Tents flapped in the
warm wind. It was time to go back. I had been home a
long time.

There was a song I heard when I was in Los Angeles by a local group. The song was called 'Los Angeles' and the words and images were so harsh and bitter that the song would reverberate in my mind for days. The images, I later found out, were personal and no one I knew shared them. The images I had were of people being driven mad by living in the city. Images of parents who were so hungry and unfulfilled that they ate their own children. Images of people, teenagers my own age, looking up from the asphalt and being blinded by the sun. These images stayed with me even after I left the city. Images so violent and malicious that they seemed to be my only point of reference for a long time afterwards. After I left.

PICADOR CLASSIC

CHANGE YOUR MIND

PICADOR CLASSIC

On 6 October 1972, Picador published its first list of eight paperbacks. It was a list that demonstrated ambition as well as cultural breadth, and included great writing from Latin America (Jorge Luis Borges's *A Personal Anthology*), Europe (Hermann Hesse's *Rosshalde*), America (Richard Brautigan's *Trout Fishing in America*) and Britain (Angela Carter's *Heroes and Villains*). Within a few years, Picador had established itself as one of the pre-eminent publishers of contemporary fiction, non-fiction and poetry.

What defines Picador is the unique nature of each of its authors' voices. The Picador Classic series highlights some of those great voices and brings neglected classics back into print. New introductions – personal recommendations if you will – from writers and public figures illuminate these works, as well as putting them into a wider context. Many of the Picador Classic editions also include afterwords from their authors which provide insight into the background to their original publication, and how that author identifies with their work years on.

Printed on high quality paper stock and with thick cover boards, the Picador Classic series is also a celebration of the physical book.

Whether fiction, journalism, memoir or poetry, Picador Classic represents timeless quality and extraordinary writing from some of the world's greatest voices.

Discover the history of the Picador Classic series and
the stories behind the books themselves at
www.picador.com